UNTOUCHED MAGIC

AN AGENTS OF MAGIC URBAN FANTASY NOVEL

SARAH BIGLOW

For information contact; www.sarah-biglow.com

Edited by: Under Wraps Publishing Services

Cover Design by: Deranged Doctor Design

ISBN: 978-1-955988-29-2

Print Published by Sarah Biglow: 2023

10 9 8 7 6 5 4 3 2 1

 Created with Vellum

NOVEMBER 15, 2019

The sun shone overhead as I stood outside the front entrance to the Boston Public Library a little before one o'clock. I checked my phone for what felt like the millionth time since I'd arrived. Normally I wasn't the type to frequent the public library, but a good friend and fellow FBI agent had made me promise to show her the sights. There was only so many duck tours a woman could stand though. Perri Fraiser, my best friend from the academy, had been detailed to a taskforce in Boston two months ago and she was due to head back to D.C.

"I am so sorry!" Perri's voice carried on the breeze as she hurried toward me on the sidewalk in a light windbreaker.

It was in the mid-fifties today. Not exactly what

I'd consider to be normal New England weather for mid-November, but I shivered at the sight of her. I tugged my jacket a little closer around my body before she pulled me into an awkward hug.

"You would think with living in a city I'd be used to the unreliability of public transportation," she said as we started for the library entrance.

"It's fine. I'm just glad we're ticking some things off your Boston sightseeing list before you head back to D.C."

"I actually wanted to talk to you about that," she said as we wound our way through the interior of the library and into the tea room for our scheduled tea time.

"You're actually staying," I replied hopefully.

"Not exactly. I put in for a transfer up here, to Agent Herrera's team full-time, but right now there are no openings. So, I just have to be patient."

Two months ago, magic had drawn Perri and I back together. She'd been undercover working to take down a human trafficking ring. The same ring that had murdered Agent Jacquie DeWitt's brother years earlier. Perri and I hadn't actually gotten to work together since then though. She'd been busy prepping for the grand jury indictment of the case. Our involvement hadn't exactly been on the books thanks to our lead coming from Jacquie's teenage niece, Neveah. She'd had a vision of her father that had led us to uncover the connection to Herrera's trafficking ring case. Until a few months ago, she'd only ever predicted the future.

"Well, I'd love for you to make your visit permanent," I said when we were ushered inside to our table. There were already little tea cakes laid out on the table along with delicate porcelain cups and matching saucers.

"There's still so much to learn here," she said, tugging off her windbreaker and slinging it over the back of her chair.

She'd become privy to my own secret during the case. The list of people who knew I had magic, but didn't have powers themselves, had rapidly expanded in the last few months. I'd always been taught that we needed to keep our abilities confidential. It was just safer that way. Though I knew I could trust Perri to safeguard my secret.

"Not sure how much I can tell you. Or show you."

"I've seen what you can do, but I know that's not even the tip of the iceberg. You said there's a governing body that oversees educating people about magic. I'd love to meet them."

"Yeah, they're not big on outsiders ... especially people without power. It defeats the whole secrecy thing."

"Right. Of course."

"Besides, magic isn't just here in Boston. It's everywhere. I bet you'll run into some magical syndicate the minute you get back to D.C. We need allies elsewhere, too."

A waiter came by and set a large teapot on the table between us before departing. Perri and I stared at the tea service for a minute before she reached out and poured herself a cup. I followed suit, but didn't drink. I wasn't a big tea person. Coffee was my preferred method of caffeine consumption.

"You guys working on anything interesting?" Perri's question caught me off guard.

"Uh, not really. Things have been pretty quiet actually." I picked up the teacup and held it gingerly between my hands. "What about you? How goes the grand jury prep?"

"Good. Herrera and the State's Attorney are confident they'll return an indictment, and we can move to trial." She took another sip of tea and reached for one of the little sandwiches on the tray between us. "So, how are things with Duncan?"

I set the teacup on the table before I dropped it.

A rush of adrenaline crashed over me and I picked up on the scent of chamomile as my magic reacted to the question. My right hand flickered from a solid state to a translucent one before disappearing up to the wrist.

Across the table, Perri's eyes widened. "Shit, sorry. Forget I asked."

I inhaled slowly through my nose and exhaled through my mouth, willing my magic to calm the fuck down. A moment later, my hand had returned to normal. My power hadn't revolted against me like that in a while. Then again, magic to some extent was tied to emotions. The stronger the emotion, the easier magic flowed.

Agent Duncan was one of the members of my team. And we'd sort of dated for a few months over the summer. I'd broken things off during the trafficking case, because I wasn't ready for that sort of commitment. At least that's what I'd told him and myself at the time.

"Kayla?" Perri's voice carried the unspoken question, 'What's wrong?'

"Things are fine." I managed through a tight-lipped smile. I even snatched up the teacup and downed the contents in one big gulp. Not very lady-like or appropriate for high tea.

"You do know I can tell when someone's lying, right?"

"He's not the problem," I finally muttered, setting the cup down in its saucer with a clink. "He's perfectly nice and cordial. Sure, I see the pining looks when he's not quick enough to hide them, but I mean we don't have any issues working together."

"So, it's Kevin?"

Before joining the FBI, I'd spent a lot of the last two years visiting Kevin Ellery in prison. His magic had turned against him, and he'd been forced to kill for a bastard named Taggart. The asshole hid behind a badge and gun for too long before the good guys had actually prevailed. But when Kevin had been released, he'd dropped me like a hot potato.

"Yes."

"Has he reached out?"

Perri didn't know the entire story about what happened with Kevin, only that we'd been together—at least I thought we had—while he was in prison and that he broke it off to find himself. I'd tried to give him the space he needed to work through his trauma. But how long was a girl supposed to wait?

"No. I've seen him around Authority Headquarters a few times, but it's not like he's texted or anything."

"I don't want to sound like a bitch, but I think he's giving you pretty clear signals he's not interested in getting back together."

I let out a groan. "I know. I think I've known that for a while now. I also know that I probably worked things up to be more than they were in my head. Ugh, it just feels so stupid."

"You are not stupid. You thought there was something there and you got a little ahead of yourself."

"I've been thinking about it a lot lately and I don't know ... maybe I was more into Kevin, because he wasn't really available. It's not like we were hooking up while he was in prison."

"And now you've got this other very attractive guy who is definitely into you and wants to be with you, that can be scary," Perri concluded.

"Hunting down bad guys and kicking ass should not be the easy part of my life," I whined.

"Life isn't supposed to be easy. I think you should call Kevin, meet up, and just once and for all put things to bed. So, you can make a clean, final break, and then decide if Duncan is worth a second chance."

I reached across the small table and grabbed my friend's hand. "This is why I need you to stick around. I'm clearly a hot mess when you're not here."

"You will be fine. Like you said, you kick ass and take down bad guys for a living." She leaned over the teapot and added in a hushed tone, "And you've got some pretty cool magic too."

I smiled as she waved her hands around in exaggerated gestures. I didn't have the heart to ruin her enthusiasm with the fact that you didn't actually see most magic being done. It wasn't meant to be flashy or obvious. Still, her over exaggeration was enough to lighten the mood and let me enjoy our time together.

Before long, the staff were ushering us out so they could set up for the final teatime at three o'clock. We made our way out of the library, and I could hear the bell at Old South Church chime across Boylston Street. The air had chilled a bit during the time we'd been inside and I caught Perri tugging on her windbreaker. I fell into step beside her, summoning just a little power.

Make it warmer.

Chamomile flared in my nose as a pocket of warm air enveloped the pair of us. Perri let out a soft gasp as she looked at me.

"Thanks."

"No reason you have to be cold if I can do something about it," I said with a shrug.

We meandered away from the library in the general direction of the Prudential Center. There were a lot of people out and about given that it was a Friday afternoon. Surprising since we weren't even that close to the Thanksgiving holiday. As we walked, I resolved to do what Perri suggested and get my love life in order. Maybe then my magic wouldn't react like I was under assault whenever either Kevin or Duncan's names came up in conversation.

"Come on, let's go this way." Perri tugged on my arm, turning us toward a street that would take us into the higher-end Newbury Street area.

We darted to the other side of the street, the walk signal had under ten seconds left to cross . I didn't spend much time in this area of town. Well, not recently anyway. Back when I'd been on the wrong side of the law, the people I'd hung out with paid visits to stores like these under cover of invisibility. We were halfway down the block when my stomach lurched. Something felt *off*.

"Why are we stopping?" Perri didn't sound overly concerned.

"There's something wrong. I need to drop the bubble," I answered. The moment I'd spoken, the bubble faded and the cooler air smacked me in the face.

It was enough to recalibrate my senses. There was something magical in the air. I wasn't as sensitive to other practitioners' abilities as some people I've known, but whatever lay ahead of us on the street was in the air enough for even the most untrained practitioner to notice.

"Wrong how?"

"There's magic. I don't know where it's coming from, but there's a lot of power and it feels like it's not friendly."

"I didn't think magic was good or evil," she reminded me.

"It's not. But whoever is working this magic, their ill intent is practically screaming at me."

"So, what do we do?"

I wanted to tell her that *we* didn't do anything. But she would never agree to bail on me. "We need to approach with caution."

My hand moved on instinct to my belt, expecting to find my holster and service weapon. Only it was empty since today was my day off. I swallowed back nerves as we walked slowly up the sidewalk. Pedestrians didn't seem to sense what was amiss. That would make it harder to get people out of the way if something went sideways.

I glanced at the storefronts of both sides of the street. Most were clothing stores with a few high-end boutiques and salons squeezed in between. My shoulders ached with tension as I pushed through the magic surrounding the area. I prayed whatever this spell was meant to do, wasn't concealing something darker.

I held a hand up to stop Perri's forward momentum. There was no reason we should be going in blind. Magic crawled just beneath my skin, itching to get out. I turned my right hand palm up and cupped it, letting the magic pool there. I mimed tossing it out into the air. *Show me what's hiding.*

There was a faint shimmer in the air before us, but nothing else changed. I wasn't wrong about whatever magic was gathering in the area. It practically pressed in against every molecule of my body. Was I strong enough to fight whatever this is? After all, I wasn't the Savior. I was just an ordinary witch, trying to do her best to keep the world safe.

"Kayla, I get that you think something is going on here, but everything looks normal to me," Perri said, disrupting my concentration.

"I'm telling you I can feel the magic here."

"Wait. Didn't you say it's everywhere, all the time?"

"Not like this. Normally, it's just kind of in the background ... ambient noise you don't even notice anymore once you're used to it. This feels concentrated, like someone purposely gathered it here. And like I said, the intent to do harm is practically smacking me in the face."

"Tell me how I can help."

"I don't know," I replied truthfully.

"Is it coming from somewhere specific?" she prodded.

I closed my eyes, trying to feel the magic with my own. Through enhanced senses I could almost feel the magic coiling in the air in front of me. I trailed a hand along the length of it, blindly following where it led. I ignored the angry horn blasts from drivers as I darted into traffic. I didn't bother to check whether Perri was behind me.

The dark magic solidified in front of me, and I opened my eyes to find myself standing across the street in front of a two-story building with a massage parlor sign in the lower window and another sign for what looked to be a doctor's office on the upper floor.

From the outside, both businesses looked unassuming, just another set of high-end establishments on the street. But the magic was definitely emanating from within one of them. If I could get a closer look at the spell, maybe I could dismantle it. I wasn't an expert, but all magic's basically like an unseen tapestry. Once you tugged on the right threads, you could undo most spells.

"Kayla!"

I turned to look at my friend. Her mouth hung open, but her words were swallowed by a sudden whoosh of hot air and a boom behind me. I slammed hard into the ground as heat cascaded down my back and everything around me turned to black.

TWO

Everything ached as the world slowly came back to me. A painful ringing in my ears hit me first. I tried to clamp my hands over my head to shut out the sound, but it only intensified it. My arms were slow to respond to my brain's command to move. Thick smoke filled the air around me. I tasted grit and ash on my tongue.

Someone approached me through the smoke and grime. My heart hammered against bruised ribs in a panic until Perri's face materialized above me. She wrapped both of her hands around my right arm and hoisted me to my feet.

"Are ... okay?" I only caught some of her words.

I took a moment to let my equilibrium settle. As

my vision cleared, I noticed the chaos around us. Civilians were running from the scene, and I could now make out the wail of incoming emergency rescue crews.

Perri kept hold of me and when she asked, "Are you okay?" The second time all of the words processed from my ears to my brain.

"What happened?" It felt like I was shouting as I pivoted slowly to see the building engulfed in flames. My neck ached and the back of my head throbbed. I pressed a hand to the base of my skull. By some miracle it came away just grimy. No blood.

"I saw smoke coming out of the window before everything just exploded," Perri finally responded.

Had magic really done this?

I tried to reach with my magic to see if the malicious intent still hung in the air. I strained to feel it. Somehow, even if someone had used magic to make a building explode, there should have been remnants of the magic still around. But I couldn't sense anything fainter than if it had happened days or even a week ago.

Glass from one of the upper floor windows shattered, raining sharp fragments to the sidewalk below. Perri and I scurried out of the way just in time to avoid further injury. I glanced up to see a man frantically trying to climb onto the tiny ledge that ran beneath the window.

Oh, shit.

"He's going to jump!" someone shouted from behind me.

"I'm going in there," I told Perri, taking a step toward the building. I thought I'd put my feelings of comparing myself to Ezri aside. Yet as I stood there, staring at the burning building, I knew she would have gone in without a second thought for her own safety. It was the right thing to do, because she was a hero. I might not be the Savior, but damn it, I could be a hero, too.

"Are you insane? You're not indestructible," she shouted.

"Fire and paramedics aren't here, and if that guy jumps, they're going to have their hands full. If there's anyone else inside, I have to try and get to them."

I moved closer to the building, waiting for the wind to pick up more smoke before summoning my power and willing myself invisible. It took longer than it should have. The magic that been so eager to track the spell not ten minutes earlier was now sluggish to respond to what I wanted.

But finally it coalesced around me, shielding me from the flames and the unbreathable air. The first floor appeared to have taken the brunt of the damage with large chunks of walls blown away. A section of ceiling hung open, exposing pipes and other systems I couldn't begin to identify. Water feebly sputtered from the sprinkler system. It did nothing against the flames leaping hungrily at the structure around me.

By some miracle, the massage parlor was empty. I checked each room, my heart skipping a beat each time I set foot in one of the small rooms, praying I wouldn't find anyone. I strained to hear what was happening beyond the building, but all I could make out was the crackle of the still-burning flames. I found the backstairs that led up to the second floor.

I tested the first step cautiously.

It held my weight. The second buckled as I moved and by the third, the wood splintered and fell away. There wasn't much chance I'd be able to get up to anyone on the upper floor. That also meant fire crews would have to approach any rescue from the front of the building.

I turned to retrace my steps to the front of the building when my magic sputtered around me. For a terrifying minute I was completely visible, susceptible to the heat and the smoke. I tried not to inhale as I groped for the exit. I knew if I took a breath, I'd devolve into coughing fits and I couldn't afford that.

"Fire department, call out!" a deep male voice boomed directly to my left.

"Here," I rasped, doing an awkward side shuffle in his direction until I felt a gloved hand on my shoulder.

A second gloved hand took hold of my arm and guided me toward the fresh air. "Come on, Miss. Let's get you checked out by the paramedics."

"There's no way to get to the second floor," I coughed as the firefighter—a woman I could just make out through her oxygen mask—turned to head back into the blaze.

"Kayla?" J.T.'s voice snapped me back to reality.

"What are the odds?" That was enough to send me into a coughing fit.

He ushered me to a gurney by a waiting ambulance and slid an oxygen mask over my nose and mouth. "Try to breathe normally."

Beneath the soot and ash caking my tongue and nose, I could almost pick up the hint of honey as he worked his literal healing magic on me. It helped. The coughing fit subsided, and the world stopped tilting off its axis.

"Thanks," I said, starting to tug off the mask.

He slid it firmly back in place. "You know, after Ezri died, I'd thought I was done with my friends acting recklessly just because they had magic to fall back on," he said.

I glanced over to see Perri nearby, phone pressed to her ear. "I don't need you ganging up on me, too."

He looked to where I pointed and gave a sad smile. "Well, maybe you should listen to your friend next time." After a moment J.T. added, "I'd ask what you were thinking, but I already know. You needed to help."

"Something weird was going on right before the explosion. There was dark magic in the air. Someone, maybe a group of someones, had put out a lot of power and it led me to the building."

A slurry of grime ran across the sidewalk as some of the firefighters who'd remained outside opened hoses, knocking down the flames from the outside. They'd also managed to rescue the man trapped on the second floor.

"At least it doesn't look like anyone died," I said before falling back into a coughing fit.

"Come on, let's get you to Boston Medical Center and have you checked out," J.T. said.

"I don't need a hospital," I protested between coughs.

"You don't have a choice," Perri said, approaching the gurney. "I just talked to Agent Cartwright and she said you need to be cleared by a doctor before you can come back."

A flash of annoyance washed over me, making me woozy. What right did she have to go over my head and call my boss? But the rational part of me knew my friend was just looking out for me.

"Okay, fine. I'll go," I said, taking shallow breaths.

"Second explosion this week," I heard one of the firefighters comment as the stream of water from the hose lost pressure now that they'd put out the flames.

I filed that away in my mind as J.T. and his partner loaded me into the back of an ambulance. Perri joined us, the doors closed, and the emergency vehicle drove down Newbury Street and through the city, sirens wailing.

I HATED HOSPITALS. I think I'd spent a lot of time hiding from the world that to be seen by so many people was unnerving. Besides, I never understood how someone was supposed to get rest in a place like this when you had nurses and doctors prodding you every hour to make sure you weren't dead.

They kicked Perri out once they'd settled me in a bay in the Emergency Room. I thought I heard a nurse insist Perri needed to be examined, too. J.T. lingered even as his partner gathered up the gurney and headed back to the ambulance bay.

"Hey, J.T.," I called, finding it easier to talk now that I didn't have an oxygen mask in the way. "Did I hear a firefighter say they'd seen another explosion like this one?"

"I think so, but I wasn't on shift when it happened. From what I heard, no one was seriously injured."

"Where was it?"

"Across the city close to the Waterfront."

"Like out near the Aquarium?"

"Somewhere out that way, yeah. But like I said, I wasn't on shift." He stepped into the area they'd curtained off for me. "What kind of magic did you feel in the air?"

"It was malevolent. But I didn't know what it was there to do, only that it wasn't good. I've never encountered anything like that before. And then, something else happened while I was in the building."

He leaned in. "What?"

"My magic glitched. Like even though I hadn't changed my intent, it just stopped working."

"Is it back to normal now?"

I raised a hand, wiggled my fingers, and watched as they disappeared one at a time. "Seems to be."

"Well, I'm not as sensitive to magic as other people, but I didn't feel anything out of the ordinary."

"That's the thing ... once the building exploded, neither did I."

"Sorry to pull you away partner, but we've got another call," J.T.'s partner said, interrupting the conversation.

"If I hear anything, I'll pass it along," he told me before following his colleague out into the main hub of the Emergency Room.

I lay there as machines beeped around me, tracking my blood pressure and heart rate and oxygen levels. With the adrenaline receding from my body, I took notice of the way my body ached from being thrown into the ground. My neck still ached when I moved it. Whiplash maybe?

I needed more information on the other

building that had exploded. My gut told me it wasn't just a coincidence. Where there was big magic, there was usually a trail leading to it. And the city had been too quiet on the magical offender front lately.

The curtain at the foot of the bed moved aside and a heavy-set nurse in pale blue scrubs stuck her head in. "There are some police officers here to talk to you, if you're up for it."

"Sure." I sat up and straightened in the bed as much as possible given that I was hooked up to so many machines.

A baby-faced officer in uniform stepped inside, notepad at the ready, followed by an older man with greying temples. He looked at me and I immediately felt uncomfortable. The irritation on his face telegraphed he was not happy to be here talking to me. Almost as if he had better things to do with his time than his job.

"Miss Rogers, is it?" the young officer said.

"Special Agent Rogers," I corrected sharply. I'd worked hard to earn that title.

"Oh, I—I uh … I'm sorry," he stammered.

"It's my day off," I sighed, feeling sorry for snapping at him. "Kayla's fine."

"So, Kayla, I'm Officer Waters and this is Detective Franz. We were hoping to ask you a few questions about what you saw today."

"Of course."

"What were you doing in the area?"

"I'd been having tea with a friend, Agent Perri Fraiser. She's not local and we went to the Tea Garden at the library."

"So, you left the library and were just, walking?" Waters continued.

"Like I said, Agent Fraiser isn't local, and I promised I'd show her the sights. We were heading down Newbury Street when we noticed smoke. It was coming from a building across the street. I went over to check it out, but before I could go inside, there was an explosion."

They wouldn't have believed me if I told them I'd followed dark magic to the scene. Hell, I wasn't sure I'd have believed it if I hadn't witnessed it myself.

"Other eyewitnesses say you ran into the building after the explosion."

I nodded, immediately regretting the movement. "There was a man on the second floor trying to climb out a broken window. I knew if he jumped, he would probably wind up with severe injuries. And that was the best-case scenario. I hoped I could reach him in time. But the backstairs collapsed before I could make it to him."

"You realize you aren't a firefighter," Franz interjected.

Yep, definitely don't like him.

"Yes, Detective. I am aware of that. But you can't honestly tell me that if you'd been on scene, you wouldn't have done the same thing? Besides, there could have been other people inside."

"And you didn't notice anything else about the scene that stood out as odd?" Waters pressed.

"No. It looked like the lower floor sustained most of the damage. But like I said, I couldn't make it up to the second floor."

"Thank you for your time." Waters handed me his card, which I tucked into my pocket. I noticed Franz didn't bother offering his. "If you think of anything else, please don't hesitate to reach out."

"You'll be my first call," I replied, plastering on a fake smile.

I watched the two men leave and settled back against the pillows. I really should ask the nurse for something for this pain, but I didn't need the side effects. There was something brewing in the city and it needed to be dealt with. The sooner we could find out what had happened at the waterfront and figure out if the fires were connected, the sooner we could snatch up the investigation and put a stop to whatever mayhem was about to unfold.

"Well, it's nice to know you can actually follow directions," Agent Cartwright said from the bay's entryway.

"Don't worry, Perri would have probably knocked me out and strapped my ass to the gurney if I'd refused," I replied, itching to tug the nasal canula out of my nostrils.

"I'm sure Perri already reminded you that you're not a superhero," she said, perching on the edge of the bed.

"I know. I just reacted."

"You did what any good law enforcement officer would have done. But Agent Fraiser did let me know that something strange happened beforehand. Something about magic." Her voice dipped to a hush on the last sentence.

I was beginning to feel like a broken record. "I picked up on some seriously powerful magic in the area. It was strong enough I could feel the intent was malicious and I think it caused the explosion. Also, I heard one of the firefighters mention this wasn't the first instance of an explosion like this. I know arson isn't our usual jurisdiction, but we need to be on this case, Molly."

"Let me do a little digging and see what I can find out first. In the meantime, you need to rest. And for the love of all that is good, try not to get blown up."

THREE

By some miracle—maybe J.T.'s magic had truly sped up the healing process—the hospital staff discharged me around nine o'clock that night. I expected Perri to be waiting for me, but instead, I found Duncan. He carried a duffel I recognized as my own go bag. Not that I needed to do much sudden travel. But it did contain a spare change of clothes and basic toiletries. An actual shower would have been better, but I'd take what I could get.

"Thanks," I said and accepted the bag. He waited outside one of the bathrooms while I changed and freshened up.

"So, where to?" He offered me a congenial smile as he led the way to his car.

"You mean to tell me you aren't under strict

instructions to drive me home and make sure I stay there?"

"I think we both know that's a pointless exercise. Molly filled me in. I know you, Kayla. You've got this in your brain. It's not going to go away until you solve it. So, why fight the inevitable?"

"Office it is."

I glanced at his reflection in the rearview mirror as he eased to a stop at a crosswalk. Perri's and my conversation from earlier played back in my head. I shouldn't broach the subject with Duncan until I'd had a chance to end things for good with Kevin. But the space between us in the car felt so loaded.

"This is probably the wrong time to mention this, but I'm planning to see my ex."

"Oh ... Okay." There was a nervous crackle in his voice.

"Not like to get back together or anything. Just to make sure we're both on the same page. I just wanted you to know that."

"I appreciate it. I think."

I drummed my fingers on the edge of the seat, needing a way to expel my nervous energy. "So, did you guys find anything else out about the other explosion? It was down by the Seaport earlier this week."

"So impatient," he chided followed by a small laugh.

The rest of the trip back to FBI headquarters felt interminable. I was convinced we hit every red light possible. I hated that I'd made it awkward between us, but couldn't figure out how to make it less tense. I was practically crawling out of my skin by the time we reached the building and parked. I was halfway to the elevators when I remembered I didn't have my gun or badge.

"Relax," Duncan whispered in my ear as he badged us through security and into the elevator.

"We got lucky no one was killed," I countered. "With the amount of power built up beforehand, I have to imagine we won't be so lucky next time."

He didn't answer as the elevator doors slid open revealing the nondescript hallway that led to our offices. The familiar sight of unused cubicles eased my nerves a little. I picked up on voices coming from the conference room and it took all of my will power not to burst into the room demanding answers. I'd run into that building wanting to be a hero, but now it felt like the universe was putting me in the path of something larger. Some magical case that I was meant to solve.

I walked in as calmly as I could to find Molly and

Jacquie DeWitt standing in front of the whiteboard. There were far too few details scribbled on it in dry erase marker. The police file that sat on the conference table behind them was thin. Neither woman looked surprised to see me.

"So, did you figure out how we get this case yet?" I blurted.

"It's only been a few hours and there's not much to go on," Jacquie replied, eyeing me warily. "It's not like magic can be listed as a cause of explosions."

"But there's got to be something that ties them together."

"Fire Investigations is still reviewing the first explosion and I'd be surprised if they get to this new one anytime soon." Jaquie gestured to the file on the table. "You're welcome to read what we've got."

I snatched up the file on the table and flipped through the meager contents from the first explosion. It had occurred at a high-end restaurant down at the Seaport around five in the morning. No one was on the premises and there were few witnesses, but it was a two-story structure. Damage appeared concentrated on the lower level.

"Can we go over there to check it out?"

"What are you hoping to find? If it's magic, this happened three days ago and last I checked even most people with magic can't pick up a trail that long after." Jacquie crossed her arms over her chest. I wondered if she realized that was the exact position she took up whenever she challenged something magical.

"There was a strange absence of magic at the scene after the explosion. Like it was building up and then just burned itself out. I don't know, maybe I'd feel that at the other scene, too?"

"I've got a friend over in Fire Investigations," Duncan offered, entering the conversation for the first time since we'd arrived. "I'm pretty sure he doesn't know about anything magical, but he might be willing to share a draft of their findings before they're official. Might even convince him to walk us through the scene."

"Great. Do it. The longer we wait, the more chance whoever is behind this gets bolder," I said.

"There isn't more we're likely to find before the morning. You need to get some sleep," Molly directed.

But I didn't feel tired. The rush of a new case was enough to reignite my adrenaline stores. "You're right. I'll get some rest. I promise."

Before leaving the conference room behind, I snapped a photo of the case file from the first explosion, making sure I had the address. I'd go home and rest, but I had a stop to make on the way. I turned to Duncan. "Mind giving me a lift?"

"I KNOW I've only driven you home a few times, but we are nowhere near your house," Duncan said twenty minutes later. "And this does not look like getting some rest."

"I told Molly I'd go home and rest. And I will. But first I'm looking for someone or something that might be able to tell us if magic was used in the area," I explained.

"And they just happen to still be in the area at almost ten o'clock at night? And they're going to talk to two feds?" Skepticism dripped from his tone.

"We won't be approaching them as feds," I answered. "Pull over here."

He did as directed, even though I caught him giving me side eye as he parked. Part of me wanted to tell Duncan to wait in the car since the person we were here to see spooked easily. But they were also part of the past I'd fought so hard to leave behind. I hated him seeing that piece of me.

"Okay, so you need to let me do the talking," I

said as I climbed out of the car, grateful for once I didn't have my badge and gun. "And leave your badge and gun in the car."

"That's not really legal," he said.

"Just trust me."

I walked down the street, eyeing the small alleyways between some of the buildings. I stopped when I felt the compulsion to turn and go back the way I'd come.

Bingo.

I pushed past the unease and stepped into the mouth of the alley beside me. "Regan, it's Kayla," I called out.

The compulsion lessened a fraction, but it still made me want to vomit when I stepped closer. Somehow, I swallowed back the bile. "I just want to talk."

The air in front of me rippled and a girl about twenty years old appeared. Her hair was done up in two buns on the top of her head straight out of an anime. For someone who lived on the streets, she could still rock smoky eye shadow and eyeliner. Her clothes were well worn and I could see bare patches in places. Her jacket was too light for the turning weather.

"You haven't been around in a while," Regan said, giving me a suspicious glance.

"I know. Things sort of got complicated after Lola."

"You're losing your mojo. Dude over there is staring at you."

I looked over my shoulder to see her pointing at Duncan. He offered a small wave. At least he'd done as I'd asked and left the badge in the car. I could still make out the bulge of his weapon beneath his jacket though. "He's a friend."

"Doesn't look like a friend." Regan shivered as a gust of wind blew around us.

"Look, I came by because I know that you know the pulse of things around here."

Regan shrugged one shoulder. "I might. Why do you and your friend care?"

"Something happened to me today and I think it affected my magic. I was wondering if anything like that might have happened around here."

"Nope." Her eyes never left the spot over my right shoulder where I knew Duncan stood.

"Regan, please. Help me out. I need to know if what happened to me might have happened to anyone else, so I can find a way to stop it."

Regan let out a sharp laugh. "You sound like that

Savior girl. And you know what happened to her, right? She got so wrapped up in trying to save people, she died."

"That Savior girl was actually a friend of mine. And she's the reason we're not all slaves to some crazy fucked up death monster."

"Oh ... Yeah, I guess that's a good thing."

"Look, I was near a building that exploded today. And I know for a fact something like that happened not far from here a few days ago. There was a huge build-up of magic right beforehand." I stepped closer and tugged off my own coat. "I know you're sensitive to that sort of thing."

Regan eyed the coat, clearly doing the mental math as to whether telling me the truth was worth a warmer coat. She didn't know I'd stashed a hundred dollars in the pocket too, as bonus. "Okay fine. But it's going to cost you."

I held out the coat. "Obviously."

She snatched it from my outstretched hand and pulled it on, sliding her hands into the pockets. Her eyes widened as she found the cash stashed inside. "I felt what you're talking about. It was nasty shit. I don't know who did it or where it came from, but it was in the air for a while. Then I heard this loud boom. I laid low after that. Too many cops."

"Did you happen to notice if the magic was still there hanging around after the explosion?"

I watched Regan as she contemplated her response. She closed her eyes and pressed her lips together in thought. "You know, now that I think about it, it did go away pretty fast. I mean you couldn't turn around without feeling it before and then it just sort of went away."

The two explosions had to be connected. "Did it mess with your magic?"

"Nah. I didn't get near the building or anything. But I've never seen magic do that before. You think it's those Order psychos again?"

"I doubt it. They've been gone for a while, and I don't think they're coming back."

Besides, most of the higher-level members didn't remember magic even existed. At least that's what I'd heard around Authority Headquarters. "Thanks for the info, Regan. I really appreciate it."

"Hey, maybe don't disappear for like half a decade next time," she called. She reached out a hand, as if to squeeze mine, but pulled it back. Time and my absence had made her distrustful.

"I'll see you around," I said and gave her a quick hug before retreating to the car. Duncan followed after me. I waited until Regan had disappeared deeper into her alley before climbing into the passenger seat.

"So, it sounds like the two explosions are linked from a magic standpoint," Duncan commented as he pulled back onto the road and maneuvered an illegal U-turn in the middle of street, heading toward my apartment.

"Not that we're going to convince the locals that they're connected in that way," I yawned.

"Well, like I said, I'll see my Fire Investigations buddy tomorrow bright and early to see what he can tell me about the first scene."

"I should go with you."

"You nearly got blown up today. I think you should relax tomorrow."

"You know that's not going to happen," I said.

"How about I make you a deal?" he said as he pulled up at a red light.

"I'm listening."

"You work through whatever hangups you've got with your ex ... and I promise as soon as I get done with my friend, I'll call you. Then we can go over whatever he's got together."

Dealing with my Kevin drama in the middle of an investigation seemed a waste of time. *It's not our investigation yet.* "Fine." I pulled out my phone and made a show of texting Kevin, asking to meet the following morning.

I didn't expect a response, much less one almost instantly. My phone buzzed with an incoming text within thirty seconds. "Guess you better hope your friend has something good to share, because I've got breakfast plans with Kevin tomorrow at nine."

Duncan cracked a smile. "Good."

"This doesn't mean that I'm ready for anything else," I said hastily.

"I know. Like I said before, I'm a patient man."

I felt heat creep into my cheeks as the light turned green and he gunned the engine. I tried to distract myself for the rest of the ride home by counting the streetlights we passed. Before I'd reached fifty, he pulled up to my apartment.

"Do I need to walk you to the door?"

"No. I'm good. I promise, I'm going to get some sleep."

"See you tomorrow."

I climbed out of the car, offered him a wave, and headed upstairs. I managed to muster enough energy to take a brief shower and clean away the rest of the grit and grime from the explosion. My muscles ached and I realized the doctor had given me a prescription for some pain medication I hadn't bothered to fill. I rooted around in my medicine cabinet, finding the bottle of pills J.T. had given me months ago. I'd only taken a couple at the time, but they had worked wonders. I could use some dreamless and healing sleep right about now. I tossed the pills back and stiffly crawled into bed.

I closed my eyes, willing the day's events not to haunt my dreams. As I tried to get comfortable, I could swear I felt that same oppressive feeling of the dark magic from the explosion pressing down around me. It knew my magic now and it wasn't going to forget me anytime soon.

NOVEMBER 16, 2019

FOUR

I woke the next morning rested, but in pain. At least I didn't feel like I was going to collapse in coughing fits anytime soon. The smoke inhalation must not have been that bad. I took a double dose of over-the-counter pain meds before heading out to meet Kevin for breakfast. He'd insisted on the Pour House. It wasn't that far from the explosion site. Maybe I could swing by the site afterward and do a little more snooping.

I pulled into a parking spot on the street and fed the meter before walking up the street toward the restaurant. I spotted Kevin sitting at one of the tables by the window when I arrived. He looked up from a menu as the door closed behind me and I slid into the seat across from him. "I didn't think this was your kind of place."

He set the menu down. "Uh, I get a discount. I work here."

I stared at him in silence. I'd been giving him so much space I hadn't even realized he'd gotten a job. I wanted to congratulate him on it, but knew it would just come across as patronizing. I knew he could do better than working minimum wage food service. But it was hard to get work elsewhere when he hadn't finished his degree and carried a criminal record.

"Oh ... I'm glad you're getting back on your feet."

"I'm looking at finishing my degree, too."

"I'm glad. It's a lot harder going back after time away than people say it is. At least, it was for me. Not that it would be for you," I rambled. God, why did I sound like a total idiot in his presence?

"Hi, folks. Oh, hi Kev," a server whose nametag read Bailey said in a chipper tone. "Can I get you something to drink?"

"Water's fine," Kevin answered.

"I'll have the same," I replied, even though in that moment I longed for something alcoholic to settle my nerves.

"Sure thing. I'll be back in a few minutes to take your order."

Kevin watched Bailey head behind the bar to put in our drink orders before turning back to me. "I know I kind of cut you out of my life. I've meant to apologize for that."

"You needed to figure yourself out. It wasn't fair of me to put my expectations on you."

"I could have handled it better."

"I think I needed time to realize some things about myself, too," I began. It was better to just get it all out before I backed down. "Like maybe I romanticized the version of you from when we were in school. And the fact that you even wanted to see me while you were inside, I got excited. But you needed a friend more than anything else."

He held up a hand to stop me. "I could have told you sooner that I didn't see the same thing between us. You're right, I needed a friend and you were there for me. But it was nice to be seen too ... as a person by someone who I knew liked me in a romantic sense."

"You weren't really available as a partner. At the time, I clung to that because I'm not really good with relationships. I don't do well with lots of attention. Never have. Still don't."

"Kayla, why did you ask me to meet you today?"

"Because I nearly got blown up yesterday and it made me realize that I can't keep looking back. The past, for better or worse, is already over and I need to move forward. I couldn't do that, in whatever form it takes, without setting things straight with you."

"Even if that means there's nothing romantic between us?"

"Even that," I agreed. "Although, I'd be open to being friends. If you're in the market for one."

"I think I might be."

Bailey took that moment to return with our waters. Her gaze stayed glued to Kevin as we placed our orders. I waited until she'd walked away before letting out a snort into my water glass.

"What?" Kevin's brow crinkled.

"That waitress. She's into you."

"We're co-workers."

"And she wants to be more than that. And unless you're her boss, I'm assuming this place doesn't care who you're dating."

"I don't know if I'm ready for anything serious like that either. I mean, she doesn't know about my past."

"It probably isn't a great conversation starter to have to explain that you were missing for five years, because you were turned into a statue."

"Yeah. That part isn't fun, either. I've been working on how to explain that to the folks in group."

"The support group that J.T. runs?"

"Yeah. It's been really good for me. I know not everyone has the same experience I did, but it's been nice to know that I'm not alone."

"I'm glad to hear it."

"But I meant more the fact that Bailey doesn't know the whole ex-con thing."

"I wish I knew how to make that all just go away." I sipped from my glass, trying to hide my discomfort. I'd never believed it was right Kevin got sent to prison for being forced to kill people.

"If it's a dealbreaker for her, then she's not the right person for me," Kevin said.

"That's a really positive outlook on it."

"So, how'd you almost get blown up?"

"Uh, just some weird magic stuff going on around the city. We're looking into it, but I can't really say much more than that."

"But you're okay?"

"Yeah ... I mean, some aches, bumps, and bruises from the blast, but other than those I'm fine. And no one died."

"I honestly don't know how you do it. I couldn't imagine having to face that sort of danger on a daily basis."

"I admit, I've got some big shoes to fill in the hero

department. I feel like doing what I am now is in some small way honoring the people who'd helped put me on this path. And if that means running into burning buildings, well then, I guess that's the price of trying to do good."

"You've come a long way from the girl I met in college, Kayla."

"I'll take that as a compliment."

Bailey returned with our food a few minutes later and slid the bill under Kevin's plate. I didn't say anything, but I had a sneaking suspicion it bore her phone number on the back. I was polite and didn't snoop.

I was halfway through my breakfast sandwich and home fries when my phone buzzed with an incoming text from Duncan. His friend in Fire Investigations had turned up something interesting.

"Sorry to cut this short, I need to go. Got a work thing. I'll see you around," I said, sliding a twenty dollar bill across the table. I was out the door before Kevin could refuse to accept the money.

I stopped for a moment when I reached the library building while heading toward Dartmouth Street. I knew Duncan would wait for me to get there to share whatever his friend had found. I could make a visit to the scene of the explosion first. But it would be easier to do it if I had an official reason to be there, rather than a witness sniffing around in the eyes of the police. I'd take Duncan with me when we were done.

Traffic toward Government Center was light once I made it back to my car and I walked into our office ten minutes later, only then realizing I hadn't responded to Duncan's text. I found him studying a document in the conference room, hands planted firmly on either side of the paper on the table in front of him.

"What's so interesting?"

My entrance made him look up, momentarily startled. "How'd it go with Kevin?'"

"Fine. We're still friends. He's got new romance drama at his job. Tell me what your Fire Investigations friend found."

Duncan cleared his throat. "So, it looks like there was some sort of incendiary device planted in the building's heating system."

So, someone set a magical bomb?

"Did they happen to find anything from yesterday's scene?"

"Not yet. But from what they could tell, the device was remote detonated."

"How did they determine that?"

"Because there was no trace of any sort of accelerant. And they confirmed the building was empty at the time of the explosion. They checked surrounding video footage, and no one entered or exited it in the hours leading up to the explosion."

"I've never heard of someone making a magic bomb, but there's a first time for everything."

"If we can find some evidence of a similar device at the second scene, we might have enough tangible nonmagical evidence to link the two scenes together and assert jurisdiction." Duncan sounded almost excited by the prospect.

"What are we waiting for?"

"Clearing it with our supervisory agents?" he deadpanned.

"We can ask for forgiveness later. Come on."

I beat him to the elevator and back down to my car. I was already starting the engine by the time he climbed into the passenger seat. "I don't love the idea of running off on our own."

"Then you can tell Molly where we're going. But I'm not waiting for permission to follow this lead."

I revved the engine, pulled out of the parking lot, and into traffic. We reached the site in what felt like no time at all. The sidewalk on either side of the structure was cordoned off by crime scene tape and I could still see damp patches on it from the fire hoses and run-off. I stopped mid-step as a wave of nausea rolled over me. For just a moment I was there laying face down on the ground, fire blazing at my back.

"Kayla, hey, maybe I should go in by myself?" Duncan's words grounded me.

I shook my head as the unease passed. "No, I'm fine."

"It's okay not to be fine all the time," he muttered, but let me take the lead as we ducked beneath the tape and approached the front of the building.

"This is an active fire scene," a male voice called from our right.

I turned, badge already in hand. "FBI," I said.

"Agent Rogers?" Officer Waters looked surprised to see me.

"Friend of yours?" Duncan whispered.

"He took my statement at the hospital," I answered as I moved to meet Waters at the crime scene tape cordoning off his side of the street. "This is my partner, Agent Evan Duncan," I introduced.

"I didn't know the FBI was involved in the case." Waters sounded nervous, like he worried he'd missed a big memo and was about to be in deep shit with his superiors.

"Well, that's why we're here. Determining if we need to offer our assistance to the Boston PD," Duncan answered before I could speak.

"Oh."

"We just wanted to take a quick look around," Duncan added. "In and out in like ten minutes, tops."

"I really should run it by my supervising officer."

"Feel free to let Detective Franz know. But we still need to get in there. We're looking at a possible serial arsonist," I said as authoritatively as I could.

Waters swallowed, those nerves showing on his young face again. "I guess it can't hurt. Just don't touch anything."

"Wouldn't dream of it," I said and clipped my badge back on my belt.

I led Duncan inside the building, my shoes squelching on the water-logged flooring and debris. It didn't smell nearly as much of ash now. The air was clearer too and I could see more of the first floor than I'd been able to the first time.

"Okay, you said there'd been some exposed pipes and other systems, right?" Duncan clicked on a flashlight and began surveying what I assumed to be the waiting area.

"I mean I didn't stop to look closely, but yeah, somewhere around there," I said, gesturing to the swath of missing ceiling.

I left Duncan to study that area and made my way back through the rest of the first floor. Carefully I assessed each room. My heart hammered just a little harder until I confirmed that there were no obvious char patterns that would indicate someone had been there and I'd missed them.

"I think I've got something," Duncan called.

I hurried back to the main room and peered at the spot where the beam of his flashlight shone. There was something small wrapped around one of the pipes. I couldn't tell if the tubing was for heating or water, but the object definitely looked like it wasn't meant to be there.

"Lift me up," I told him, moving to position myself in front of him. I pulled on a pair of gloves while I waited.

He didn't question. Instead, he just hoisted me up by the waist, so I could get a better look. It was definitely something that didn't belong, but I also didn't see how it could have set the fire.

"Is this what the other device looked like from the first scene?" I called down.

"I think so." I tugged my phone free from my pocket and snapped a photo of it, so we could at least compare the devices when we got back to the office.

That would be enough for Molly to step in to assist the local law enforcement. Though it didn't explain how the hell it set off two explosions. I called up my magic, trying to probe the device. The soothing scent of my own magic filled my nose and sharpened my vision. I could see where it was hooked into the existing system and I could feel just the barest hint of magic around it. It carried that same odd feeling, like it was days or even weeks' old magic. But it was definitely the same power I'd felt before the blast.

"I think we've got enough to go back to Molly," I confirmed.

"After you," Duncan said with a gesture toward the front of the building.

When we emerged, Detective Franz stood behind Officer Waters. The poor officer looked terrified. I locked eyes with Franz for a moment before addressing Waters as I pulled off my gloves. "Thank you, Officer Waters for your assistance. We'll be in touch."

"You can't just let anyone who shows up go traipsing through an active scene," Detective Franz chastised the young man in front of him.

"He was deferring to a superior officer," Duncan said, stepping in to defend the officer.

I ducked under the other side of the crime scene tape and marched back to the car, waiting for Duncan to follow me. In short order, we'd left the two police officers behind.

"That guy is a piece of work," Duncan commented as we neared FBI Headquarters.

"That's one way to put it," I snickered.

When we walked into the conference room five minutes later, both Molly and Jacquie were waiting for us. "I hope you slept," Molly said, eyeing me.

"I did. We've got news, too." I nudged Duncan in the ribs, but he made a gesture for me to continue. "We confirmed the two explosions are connected. There were similar incendiary devices at both scenes that I think were likely triggered by magic. We need to be on this case."

Molly turned to Jacquie. "You ready to head back to your old stomping grounds?"

It hadn't even occurred to me that Jacquie's former division in the police department was the one leading the charge on these investigations. I knew she was a respected cop before joining the Bureau. I just hoped her presence would quell any hurt feelings about us swooping in on their case.

"Just don't expect a warm welcome," Jacquie said as she picked up her phone and made the call.

FIVE

Like Jacquie predicted, the local department's boots on the ground were less than thrilled to see us walk in half an hour later. Jacquie led us to the captain's office where the four of us crammed in across the desk from Captain Beech.

"You mind explaining again how you know there's a connection between these two scenes when Fire Investigations hasn't even had a chance to review the second scene?" Captain Beech's tone made Jacquie stand ramrod straight.

"We have reason to believe they were set by the same offender," Jacquie said.

"Yes, I got that from your call, DeWitt."

Jacquie cast a furtive glance my way before she exhaled. "Also, we picked up on some magic at the second scene and we have eyewitnesses who confirmed the presence of similar power at the first scene."

"I see why you couldn't tell me that over the phone."

I stared at the woman, mouth agape. Ezri had never mentioned the Captain knew about magic. From what I'd seen, even as an infrequent outside observer, Ezri had kept our secret tightly controlled at work. But the way Jacquie just dumped the truth on her and she didn't even blink made my head spin.

Captain Beech looked at me. "I'm guessing you didn't know that I knew. You're not the first person to react that way." The smile she'd put on faltered for a moment. "All right, I'm fine with you taking point on this."

"Any of your guys going to buck at us for swooping in?" Molly asked.

"Detective Franz was not pleased to see us this morning at the second scene," I offered.

Captain Beech snorted. "I'm not surprised. He's not happy to see most people in general. But I'll keep him in line."

"Then we better get set up," Molly said and started for the door.

I caught Captain Beech give Jacquie a meaningful look and I could only assume it had something to do with Ezri. She might have been gone for nearly two years now, but her presence was still felt in all the places she'd touched.

The conference room was smaller than the one in our office, but it already had the two case files waiting for us with a map of both locations hanging on one wall. I picked up the file on the first explosion, studying it again and hoping I'd missed something on the first pass.

"Did anyone interview the restaurant owner?" I asked the room at large.

"We've had a hell of a time finding them," Officer Waters said from the doorway. "But I can get you the address."

"Thanks."

"What about the building from yesterday?" Duncan added.

"We haven't been able to get in touch with the owner of the massage parlor. The therapist whose office was on the second floor is still in the hospital," Waters answered. He stepped into the room, leaning in almost conspiratorially. "Did you know this was a serial case? Is that why you were there when it happened?"

"Wrong place, right time," I answered.

"Agent DeWitt and I are going to talk with the restaurant owner. You two pay a visit to the therapist in the hospital. If we can figure out what might connect the two besides the manner of attack, we might have a chance to stop this before it goes any farther," Molly instructed.

"You didn't even give us a chance to figure this out!" Detective Franz's voice carried from the bull pen.

"Last time I checked, Detective, I was the one who made the decisions on whether to bring in help on cases. Not you. Now, you either play nice, or you're off the case entirely."

I couldn't help but laugh at the dressing down. Somehow, I managed to cover it up with the folder containing the therapist's name. I caught Duncan smile a little too as we headed for the parking lot.

THE THERAPIST, Dr. Benjamin Abbott, was in a private room, sitting by the window when we arrived. I knocked on the doorframe to get his attention.

"Dr. Abbott?"

He turned at the sound of his name and straightened a little. "Yes. Can I help you?"

"I'm Agent Rogers and this is Agent Duncan. We're with the FBI. We're investigating the explosion that happened at your office yesterday."

His brow knit together as his eyes focused on me. "You were there."

"I was." I moved to the table and pulled the other chair out. "Mind if I sit?"

"Sorry, of course. My head's still a bit fuzzy from everything."

"Last I saw, you were trying to climb out a second story window," I noted.

"Panic, I guess. Thankfully, the fire department got there."

"Can you tell me what you remember about what happened?"

Dr. Abbott rubbed at the scruffy five o'clock shadow on his cheeks and chin. "I was getting ready for a patient. Thank God they were running late. And then, out of nowhere, there was this sort of hissing sound followed by a loud boom. Before I knew it everything was in flames."

"Do you remember where the hissing sound came from?"

He scrunched his eyes shut. "I think it came from the floor. But that doesn't make sense."

"There are pipes that run under your floor, in the ceiling of the business below," I noted. "I saw them when I was inside."

"Oh, right. They weren't there, were they?"

"No, it didn't look like they were open," I answered.

"Good." His posture relaxed and I could swear I caught a hint of something like cantaloupe wafting from him.

Does he have magic?

I leaned on the edge of the table and produced my phone. I pulled up the photo of the device I'd taken at the scene earlier and slid it across the surface. "We found this hooked into the pipes."

He made a good show of studying the image, pressing his fingertips to the screen to enlarge the image. "I've got no idea what that is."

"A lot of the damage appeared contained to the first floor. But I'm guessing you share things like plumbing and heating, right?"

"Yes. We split the utilities. They pay water and I pay electricity. We have our own Wi-Fi networks."

"Do you know if there's been any work done recently in the building?" Duncan interjected, moving from where he'd been loitering by the door in the hospital room.

Dr. Abbott tilted his head to one side in thought. "We had some issues a couple months back with the air conditioning not working."

"Did you call for the repair?" I asked, taking my phone back.

"No. I was actually on vacation around the time. Marta, the woman who owns the massage parlor downstairs texted me to tell me about it. She said she found a guy to take care of it. I didn't think anything of it other than making sure I paid her for half the invoice."

If someone had been in the system months ago, maybe whatever the device was had simply gone off by error? For all we knew it was meant to regulate some system I didn't understand. "And there's been no other work done in the building since that you can think of?"

"Not that I remember."

That cantaloupe smell wafted toward me again as Dr. Abbott fidgeted in his seat. His fingers clamped around the edge of the table like a vice.

I cleared my throat. "This is going to sound like a strange question, but did you happen to feel any sort of pressure build up before the hissing sound?"

"I'm not sure I understand what you mean."

"I mean, magic."

He blinked at me, before his gaze narrowed to really take me in. "What did you say your name was again?"

"Agent Kayla Rogers."

"Forgive me, this may sound strange, but did you know Desmond Fellowes?"

Hearing Desmond's name come out of this stranger's mouth caught me off guard. "I did. He was a good friend, something of a mentor."

Dr. Abbott's gaze grew wistful, unfocused. "We were colleagues. Before he went off and joined the police, that is."

"So, I take it you're in the know about magic?"

Abbott glanced in Duncan's direction. "From your casual use of the term, I take it we aren't in mixed company?"

"I don't have any powers, but I know the basics," Duncan answered.

"I'm a witch. Well, I suppose technically I'm a Whisperer. My magic went a little uh haywire a few years back and Desmond was kind of my lifeline."

"Desmond told me about you," Abbot said, turning his attention back to me. "Years ago. A young Whisperer who he'd helped out, turned her life around. I didn't realize you'd joined law enforcement, too."

"This was a recent career change. After we lost him and ... well, it felt like the right thing to do. To put my skills to good use."

"I know he would have been proud. He was a good man. I was so sorry to hear about his passing."

"It was a shock to everyone. No one expects the guy behind the desk to take a bullet in the line of duty."

An awkward silence fell between us. I longed to fill it with more questions about his connection to Desmond, but this wasn't the time to go digging into the past. Across the table, Dr. Abbott shifted in his seat. After a moment, his smile dipped into a frown. "Do you think someone targeted us?"

"It's possible. We're investigating a similar explosion across the city. Do you know of anyone who might have had a grudge against you or your downstairs neighbor?"

"No. Nothing like that. Our businesses are relatively small. Our client bases are pretty constant."

"No new faces recently? No angry complaints you might have heard about?"

"No. I haven't been accepting new patients for a while. I'm comfortable with the roster I've got. I just can't imagine why anyone would do something like this. I help people."

"Magical people?"

"The occasional Authority member. But my practice is mostly mundane folks."

"How do people find out about you, from our community, I mean?"

"For a while, I had a flyer posted at Authority Headquarters. But I took it down when I stopped accepting new patients."

"Doctor, do you feel that your abilities give you an edge in your practice? Something that someone might take offense to." Duncan's question made me turn to look at my partner.

"How do you mean?"

I think I knew what my partner was getting at. "Desmond was good at doing guided memory walks as a way to help a patient go through and heal from trauma," I explained.

"I see. A lot of what I deal with is couple's counseling. Family therapy. I do have a knack for pinpointing stressors, but I don't think it has anything to do with my magic. Desmond was particularly gifted in the way he used his abilities."

Before I could say anything more, a nurse appeared in the doorway. "Sorry to interrupt, but it's time to check your vitals, Dr. Abbott." She wheeled a portable blood pressure checker into the room and wrapped it around his right arm. She slid a pulse oximeter onto his left index finger.

I tugged a business card from my pocket and slid it across the table before she held a temporal thermometer to his forehead. "If you think of anything, please call."

"Thank you."

Duncan led the way out of the room and back to where we'd parked. I slid into the passenger seat as he got behind the wheel.

"You, okay?" The concern in his voice made me smile.

"Yeah. I just wasn't expecting to hear Desmond's name today. It makes sense, I guess. It would be ridiculous to think he was the only magical shrink out there."

"I wonder if any of the other businesses were owned by magical folks," Duncan offered as he pulled into the flow of traffic.

"You're thinking this is magically motivated."

"Well, from what you said there was some massive build-up of magic before each explosion. I'm betting there's got to be some connection. It feels like too big of a coincidence otherwise."

He wasn't wrong. But if the device had been put in place months ago, why trigger it now?

"What I don't get is why now? I mean, if I'm trying to target someone and they've pissed me off enough for me to set a magical explosive inside their building, I'm not going to wait months to trigger it. I'm going to want to cause as much damage as soon as I can to make myself feel better," I pondered.

"That is the question of the hour," Duncan agreed. "Was there anything you could sense at the scene, like how long the magic had been building?"

"No, and to be honest, I've never really used my magic to figure something like that out. I wouldn't know where to start."

"Do you think it would make sense to contact some of your more magically inclined associates to see what they might be able to figure out?"

"Until we have more to go on, I don't think it makes sense to bring anyone else in yet." Besides, I wasn't even sure if we *had* someone who could handle magical bombs.

As we made our way back to the police precinct, my phone pinged with an incoming text. I glanced at the screen long enough to read a message from Perri apologizing for bailing on me at the hospital. Agent Herrera had called her back in for something to do with the grand jury. I sent a reply letting her know I was fine and working a case of my own. A knot of tension I hadn't realized was ratcheting up between my shoulder blades eased. I'd been so focused on diving into the case, I hadn't acknowledged that my friend had bailed on me without a word. At least now I knew the reason.

"Everything okay, Kay? You got quiet there for a minute."

I looked at Duncan. "Sorry, I'm fine. It was just Perri checking in and apologizing for bailing at the hospital." After a beat, I continued. "I'm going to let Molly know we're on our way back. Hopefully they've found a lead we can use with the restaurant owner."

As we neared our destination, I couldn't help but wonder how exactly someone would create a magical bomb. Also, how close would they need to be to set it off? The amount of power I'd felt suggested they could have been at least a block away. Getting available video footage was just another thing I added to my mental list of things to do. Besides, we needed to know if Molly and Jacquie had found anything similar with the restaurant owner—if they were magical and if they'd had work done. And I couldn't shake the feeling that whoever was behind this was just getting started.

Weekend traffic picked up as we made our way back to the precinct. We pulled into a parking space a little before noon. I spotted Molly's car a few rows over. Hopefully that meant we'd have good news waiting for us. The precinct conference room was devoid of uniformed officers. Even Detective Franz was nowhere to be seen.

"Where's our favorite detective?" I asked Jacquie.

She smirked. "Captain Beech sent him to hunt down the owner of the massage parlor."

"Oh, I'm sure he was thrilled," I replied with a laugh.

"You two get anything from the therapist?"

I had to swallow the sudden lump in my throat at

her question. "Yeah." I glanced at the doorway, preferring to fill her and Molly in at the same time to save from repeating myself. "He knew Desmond. I guess they were friends or at least ran in the same magical therapist circles."

"Oh. So, your guy had magic, too, then."

"He did. I could pick up a faint scent of it. But he said he didn't really use it in his sessions." After a beat, I asked, "So, the restaurant owner had magic, too?"

"Yes. Not that she was thrilled to admit it to two mundane agents."

"Oh please, you two have done more for the magical community than most people."

"I appreciate you saying that. Sometimes it's hard being on the outside." An awkward silence fell between us before she gave a curt nod and said, "What else did you find?"

"We also got confirmation that a few months back someone came in to do work on the air conditioning system," I explained. "So, it's possible whoever is responsible either used that time window to stash the device and conceal it with magic or—"

"Or they put it there."

"Right." Neither option thrilled me. But I still didn't understand the prolonged waiting period between setting the device and using it. "Did the restaurant owner mention anything about having work done on the building recently?"

"She mentioned they had some venting issue in their kitchen." Jacquie turned to the conference table and flipped through some images I recognized from the first case file and the Fire Investigations initial report. "It looks like they found the device in the kitchen."

"Okay, so we've got someone who is targeting magical businesses," I said, feeling energy begin to crackle through my body. We were starting to get somewhere.

"It would appear that way. Although with the second attack we can't be sure the first floor wasn't the target," she reminded me.

"We have an easy way to figure that out," I said as an idea hit me.

"We do?"

"A few months back, when we were working the human trafficking case, I asked J.T. to get in touch with the Council and get me records of everyone on the Authority's radar. We just need to cross-reference the massage parlor owner with that list."

It wasn't a perfect solution, because there was a possibility the owner could still be magical and not in the Authority's files, but it was worth a shot. And I could always pay Dr. Abbott another visit in the hospital to see what he knew about his downstairs neighbor.

"It's worth a try," Jacquie agreed. "And we may want to touch base with Avery. She might have some idea of how these devices could be set to work."

"Let's go," I said, starting for the door. "We can get the files J.T. sent over a few months ago from FBI headquarters before we head out to Newton."

"You can fill Agent Cartwright in on the way."

I took a step toward the door when the world tilted sideways and my balance faltered. My body suddenly ached and I barely managed to grab hold of the back of a chair to keep me steady.

"Whoa," I groaned, shutting my eyes to try and fight off the dizziness.

"What's going on?" Jacquie's voice came from beside me. I could feel her hand on my elbow, guiding me to a seated position.

"I'm fine," I lied. "I think I just moved too fast."

"You were nearly blown up, Kayla. You need to take some time and heal."

I opened my eyes again. "This is a magical problem. Last I checked, I'm the only one on this team with magic. You can't sideline me."

"I'm not benching you. But you need to take care of yourself. As you rightly pointed out, Molly and I are damn good at our jobs and we are more than capable of liaising with the Council to get what we need."

"But sitting at home is just going to make me go stir crazy," I protested.

Her lips pressed into a firm line and she studied me for a long moment. "Fine. But I am taking point. Got it?"

"Yes, Ma'am."

BY THE TIME we'd swung by our office to retrieve the list and were on our way to Authority Headquarters, the fatigue and pain had subsided some. It didn't stop Jacquie from glancing at me every thirty seconds to make sure I wasn't going to keel over. The Authority building soon rose up in front of us with its empty circular drive waiting.

"Have you been by recently?" I asked as conversationally as I could.

"I've been bringing Troy and Neveah by on the weekends when Denise is working. But I don't usually stay."

"How are they doing?"

"Good. I think Neveah is finally in control of her powers and knowing what really happened to her dad helped bring them all a sense of peace."

"Yeah, I bet."

"What about you?"

I shook my head. "I've kind of been avoiding it, if I'm honest."

"Any particular reason?"

"Oh, you know, guy drama." Although, I didn't have that for an excuse anymore. "But I think I'll be around more now. I don't know ... maybe I can help steer some young practitioners away from ending up like I did."

"Being around them might be good for you, too," she commented as we headed inside.

I let Jacquie take the lead up to the second floor. I could hear muffled voices coming from within the Council chamber. We might be FBI, but we didn't have a right to barge in on their meeting. So, I busied myself skimming through the records J.T. had handed over a few months ago looking for the massage parlor owner's name.

Nothing came up.

"I should swing by to confirm, but it doesn't look like she's magical. My guess is if Dr. Abbott was the target, they used the easier first floor access to get what they needed."

"Seems reasonable," Jacquie agreed as the doors opened, and semi-familiar faces appeared. They gave us polite nods as they dispersed.

When the last person had exited, I stepped into the room and made way through to the short hallway leading to the tech hub. I expected to find Avery sitting there in front of her many screens, headphones slung around her neck like a fashion statement only she could pull off. Instead, a balding guy whose name I thought was Morgan had taken up residence. I cast Jacquie a skeptical look before rapping my knuckles on the doorframe to get his attention.

He spun in his chair. "What do you—" his gaze traveled to our prominently displayed badges as he stood up and said, "Can I help you officers?"

"It's Agents," I corrected. "And we're actually looking for Avery."

"She just stepped out, so she's not here."

"Really? I thought she'd finally learned to turn invisible," I replied, my tone dripping with snark.

"Don't joke about that. It really happens to people," Morgan said.

I couldn't resist an eye roll. "I'm well aware."

After taking a breath to get my attitude in check, I said, "Do you know when she'll be back? It's important."

"Think she went to get lunch, so it could be a while. Maybe I can help?"

As tempting as it was to get answers now, Morgan wasn't vetted by the Bureau. Avery was an official consultant and cleared to deal with our cases. He wasn't and letting him have access to the information would jeopardize any legal case we tried to bring later against our culprit.

"We'll wait," I answered.

"Suit yourself," he replied and turned back to his computers.

We retreated to the Council chamber, and I sunk into one of the chairs to wait. Jacquie stood beside me. She pulled up something on her phone and scrolled through. Silence filled the air between us until she looked up and said, "If you were going to make something like this, how would you do it?"

"Uh ... I wouldn't be stupid enough to try something so obviously dangerous."

"Humor me."

"I don't know. I mean, imbuing objects with magic takes a lot of power from what I've heard."

"Strong bloodlines," Jacquie said with a small nod to herself.

"But the only people we know with powerful enough magic to maybe do something like that are dead," I added.

"Correction, people with strong enough good magic."

"Anyone who had any power on the other side is long gone."

"Setting aside that issue, if you had the power, how would you craft it. Like you said, it appears these devices were set weeks to months ago, but only triggered now. So, how would you get that to work?"

The door to the room opened and Avery walked in, a bag slung over one shoulder. Her trademark headphones were missing from around her neck. "Please tell me no one's dead."

"For once, no," Jacquie replied. "Or missing for that matter."

"Then is it too much to hope this just a social visit?"

"Afraid not. We've got a case we could use your thoughts on," I answered and stood up. "But, uh, you're going to need to kick your buddy out in there. He's not cleared for this."

Avery gave a small smirk before walking past us. "Give me a minute."

I could hear muffled voices from within the tech hub as Avery kicked Morgan out. He shuffled past us a moment later looking browbeaten and perhaps a little jealous. I waited until he was well beyond the Council chamber before heading in.

"So, what's going on?" Avery sat in the seat Morgan had occupied on our arrival.

"We've had two explosions in the city. Both appear to be targeting businesses run by practitioners. And we're pretty sure magic was used to detonate them," I explained in one long breath.

"You said no one died." Her voice carried a note of disbelief.

"Luckily, no one did. But we're trying to figure out how the device works. Or where you might find information on how to create something like this," Jacquie interjected.

"I mean, you can find pretty much anything on the dark web if you know where to look," Avery answered.

"We're pretty sure whoever made them had to be pretty powerful to imbue objects with that much firepower," I continued.

"It's possible. I mean, if you build it with the

right intent, you could probably have it pull power from somewhere else."

"Like where?"

"I don't know. Look, give me a little time to see what I can dig up online."

"Great, just call when you find something."

Jacquie started for the door when Avery made a guttural noise, like she wanted to say something, but stopped herself. Jacquie arched a dark brow at her. "Something wrong?'

Avery looked at me. "The last time you came to me for help, I told you I wouldn't always be around to be your tech guru."

"Yeah, so?"

"Well, I think this might be the last time I can help you."

I wanted to protest, but words failed me. I didn't have a right to demand she keep working with us. She wasn't an employee. She was free to do what she pleased. But it had been easier diving into cases knowing we had someone we could trust with the technical aspects that arose.

"Are you going somewhere?" Jacquie sounded unsure of her words.

"If I were talking to anyone else, I'd say you'd probably think I was crazy. But last week, I had this really vivid dream. Desmond came to me and he told me that something was coming, a destiny he couldn't have foreseen. And I need to be ready to embrace it."

"Well, when your dead husband tells you to get ready for something life-changing, you better listen," I said and laughed, trying to lighten the mood.

"It's time," she replied. "I came here looking for my place and for a while, I found it here with the Authority and with Des. And I helped people. But lately, I've felt like there's something missing in my life. I thought it was just grief for a while, but I think I've finally reached a point where I can let myself move on." She plucked her glasses off and dabbed at the corners of her eyes.

"You deserve happiness and fulfillment," Jacquie said.

"I don't know what's in store for me, but whatever it is, I know that Des would want me to follow it with everything I've got. So, I will help you figure out who is making magic bombs, but after that, I need to get ready to start the next chapter of my life."

I closed the distance between us and pulled her into a hug. She stiffened for just a second before she relaxed and returned the embrace. "I'll miss you."

"I'm not gone yet," she replied and pulled free. She dabbed at her eyes again and settled her glasses back on the bridge of her nose. "Look, I'll need at least a few hours to see what I can find about your bombs. Anything you can send me from the case files would help narrow the search."

Jacquie held up her phone. "I've sent you what we have."

"Thanks. How about we meet tonight at nine at Notre Dame and I'll share what I find?"

"You really think talking about it out in the open is a good idea?" I quipped.

"I can't think of a safer place. With the wards Jonathan put up, no one is going to be eavesdropping on us."

"See you tonight then."

Just then, my phone buzzed with an incoming call from an unknown number. I excused myself into the next room and answered. "Agent Rogers."

"Agent, it's Dr. Benjamin Abbott." I picked up on the strain in his tone. It hadn't been present when we'd spoken this morning.

"Is everything okay?"

"You told me to call if I thought of anything. Well, I haven't exactly, but something happened that I thought you should know about."

"I'm listening."

The line was quiet for a few moments. I pulled

the phone away from my ear to check I hadn't lost the call. The screen still showed an active call. "Hello? Dr. Abbott, are you still there?"

"Yes. Sorry, but I think you need to come here. It's just that, there's something wrong with my magic."

SEVEN

When we arrived at the hospital, we found Dr. Abbott pulling on his jacket with discharge papers tossed on the end of the bed. He looked up at our arrival and I caught the tension tightening the muscles in his neck.

"You need to explain exactly what you meant by something is wrong with your magic," I said, barring his ability to leave the room.

"You can speak freely. I'm a former associate of Desmond Fellowes, too," Jacquie noted.

Abbott slid his jacket off and sunk to the bed. "It's hard to explain, but it feels like my magic is spotty."

I flashed back to the burning building where my magic had fizzled out without me dropping the spell to hide myself. "It's there, but you try to do a spell and it doesn't work?"

He nodded. "And when I could get it to take, it didn't last long."

"I experienced something similar at the scene, not long after the blast," I admitted. "We believe that whoever set these devices used magic to trigger them. We're not quite sure yet what sort of spell was used, but it's entirely possible the aftermath is messing with powers, too."

"So, it's not permanent."

"I wish I could give you an answer. Maybe give it a few days of rest and see. It could also be stress relat-ed." Please let it just be a stress reaction.

"If you think the attack was magic based, you must think I was the target."

"We certainly aren't ruling it out. From what we could gather, we don't believe your downstairs neighbor has magic."

"No. She's normal. Oh, God ... has anyone been able to reach her?"

"The police are on it," Jacquie said calmly. "We appreciate you bringing this to our attention. Given we need to pursue all angles, if you were the target, then perhaps someone you've seen in a professional capacity could be involved?"

"Agent, I'm sure you know that telling you about any of my patients would violate doctor-patient confidentiality."

"If that patient was a danger to themselves or others, then it doesn't apply and you have an obligation to disclose that information," Jacquie countered.

"We're not interested in your mundane patients. You said you treated a few Authority members. No one comes to mind?"

"Like I said, most of my clients are mundane. I haven't seen anyone with magic in a while." He cleared his throat. "Most of my files were in my office. But I'll see what I have at home. I honestly can't think of anyone who would want to target me like this."

"You've got my card. It has my email address on it. Send over whatever you can find that you think might be relevant," I instructed.

A knock on the doorframe drew our collective attention to a scrub-clad nurse. "Sorry, we need to turn over the room."

Dr. Abbott put on his jacket and folded up the paperwork from the end of the bed, stowing it in his pocket. I noted the clothes he now wore were different from the ones he'd been brought in yesterday. Someone must have brought him a change of clothes. Hopefully that same someone was waiting to drive him home.

"I'll do what I can," he said before leaving Jacquie and I standing in the room.

There was something about the way Dr. Abbott had reacted to the fact I didn't think his magic was completely gone that felt familiar. I couldn't place it, no matter how hard I tried as we made our way back to the car. We still had most of the afternoon and evening before we were set to meet with Avery.

"What's on your mind?" Jacquie didn't even need to make eye contact from her spot behind the wheel for me to sense her inquisitive stare.

"I'm not sure. Something about the way he reacted feels like it should be forming a connection in my head, but I'm not making it."

"Give it some time. Whatever it is will come to you. Besides, I'm pretty sure he just lied to us."

"You think he knows who might be out for him?"

"If not the exact person, he's got a few potential candidates."

"I get he wants to protect his patients, but someone just tried to kill him. You'd think he'd be more willing to help."

"My guess is he's scared. Like you said someone tried to kill him with magic. And it nearly worked."

I couldn't blame him for being scared. But maybe if we brought up a suspect, he'd be able to confirm or deny the possibility. "Was there any video footage out by the restaurant?"

"Good thinking," Jacquie said and tapped the screen of her phone in the center console, bringing up Molly's number.

"You on your way back?" Molly answered.

"We've got some potential leads. Kayla's got a good idea. We need to check video footage at the first scene."

"Not the day of the incident, though. We need footage for the day that they had repair work done on their kitchen vents," I added hastily.

"It's worth a shot," Molly agreed.

"We're also meeting Avery tonight. She's tracking down any possible information and connections on the dark web for creating these kinds of devices," I continued.

"Good work. We've managed to confirm with the massage parlor owner that she handled the repairs for the cooling system two months ago. She's going to see if she's got an invoice for the company. She also confirmed neither she nor any of her employees were there when the building exploded."

With any luck, both buildings were serviced by

the same company. Even if we figured out the way in which the devices were planted, it didn't explain why these particular targets were bombed. I could see a disgruntled patient perhaps, but why target a restaurant at the waterfront?

"Has anyone been able to make any connections between the two targets?"

"Duncan is pulling what he can on the owners, but so far, aside from them being magical, there's nothing obvious. They don't run in the same circles. So, we're at a dead end there."

Maybe Avery could give us something that might point to a group or person that linked the attacks. Now we just had to wait.

THE LINE OUTSIDE NOTRE DAME—THE only magical bar in Boston—at eight forty-five was practically anemic. I'd never seen it only reaching the end of the building in all the years I'd been coming. It usually snaked down the block. Jonathan's usual bouncer stood at the door with beefy biceps crossed over his chest as I approached with Jacquie, Molly, and Duncan in tow. He eyed our badges still on prominent display.

"The boss knows you're coming?"

Molly held up her phone. "He does now." Her phone dinged with an incoming message, and she waved it in the man's face. "And he says come right in."

"You're giving him a bad reputation," the bouncer muttered before we headed inside.

Duncan gave me a confused look and I snickered. "Jonathan doesn't like law enforcement. Why he's dating an FBI agent, I couldn't tell you. But the more we come in, the less street cred he's got for being a badass."

"He's dating me, because *I* am a badass," Molly said just loud enough for me to hear above the thump of the bass on the dance floor.

Despite the meager crowd outside, the dance floor was packed. There were open seats at the bar and some of the high top tables were vacant. Some limited seating in the back was available, too. I spotted Jonathan behind the bar, mixing drinks and setting a tray of beer bottles out for one of the few servers to bring by.

I scanned the tables for Avery, but didn't see her yet. The rest of the quartet had moved to the far end of the bar where there was more room to stand. I hurried to join them.

"You want something to drink?" Jonathan's voice cut above the music and made me jump.

"We're working," Molly answered, leaning her elbows on the bar. She rested her chin in one hand. "But I appreciate the offer."

"I thought we had an agreement. No more working in my bar."

"Oh, come on ... we're just meeting a friend to exchange some information. Nothing flashy."

"Humph." The smile on his lips countered the sound of disapproval.

Jacquie moved to claim one of the round tables in the back and Duncan dragged over an extra chair, so we'd be ready when Avery arrived. I settled into one of the seats close to him. "I can't decide if I want Avery to find something or not," I practically shouted over the music.

He didn't have a chance to answer before Avery appeared, elbowing her way through the crowd on the dance floor. She cast Jonathan a look—one I assumed meant he'd let her in without paying the cover just like us—before throwing herself into one of the empty seats. Jacquie and Molly filled the remaining seats before Molly looked at me.

"Is there any way you can make it easier to hear?"

I bit back the retort about asking her boyfriend to do it. "I can try, but my magic has been a little off since yesterday."

"I've got it," Avery said. She closed her eyes and a pale light spread out around us, insulating our conversation from the rest of the bar and keeping the noise outside.

"So, what did you find?" I leaned in on the table, even though the space around us had quieted.

"A lot of shit I never wanted to know. But from the information you sent over, it looks like the device itself is pretty simple and definitely homemade. You could probably buy most of the parts at a big chain home furnishing store, or maybe an auto shop."

"What about the magic?" Molly pressed.

"So, from what I could find, there are few people who talk about using magic as a trigger. It sounds like there are two ways to do it. The first, you just pour a whole lot of anger and hate into your spell, amping it up. Most of what I found said you've got a short window of time to get clear. Twenty minutes maybe."

"That doesn't fit with when we think the devices were planted."

"Right. There was one other way that I found. The spell itself is designed to pull bits of magic over

time to build toward a critical mass and then it trig-
gers a reaction."

"I thought there's magic everywhere. So,
wouldn't the device just existing have the same
effect??" Jacquie said.

"Not exactly," Avery answered. "Yes, technically
there is magic everywhere, but it's not being used.
That's the key. It has to be in use to affect the accu-
mulation."

"I felt a lot of magic building up before the
explosion yesterday," I said and glanced at Jacquie.
"Maybe Dr. Abbott was lying about more than just
having a hunch about our culprit?"

"Could be."

"Where was it?" Avery adjusted her glasses.

"Downtown, near Newbury Street."

"It's possible that there was just enough magic
being done in the area that it built up sufficiently to
detonate."

"Is there any way to set how long it should take
to go off? I mean magic does fade with time," I
noted.

"You'd need a limit on how long it would last
before it just wouldn't work anymore," Avery
confirmed.

"Would a couple months be too long?"

"Not if whoever was behind the original spell was strong enough."

We were back to trying to find powerful practitioners. As helpful as it was to have an explanation of how these bombs worked, it was still frustrating to be no closer to having a name or a face for the bomber. And we still didn't have a clear reason for why.

"I wish I could be more help, but that's all I could find," Avery said.

"You didn't find anyone talking about this recently?" Duncan probed.

"Most of the posts were at least six months old. I didn't see any repeat names across the boards I searched either."

"Thanks. It was a worth a shot," he sighed.

Around us, the gauzy haze of Avery's spell blinked out of existence. The surprise on Avery's face signaled she hadn't meant to do it. Was my spotty magic contagious now? The shift in decibels made my eardrums ache and the bass beat throbbed in my temple.

By the bar, Jonathan looked around and for a split second the magic he used to glamor himself as looking normal flickered. I'd never seen the man even remotely scared before. Annoyed or pissed off, sure. But never afraid. The look of terror on his face should have been all the warning I needed that something was truly wrong.

Above the music and ambient noise of nearly one hundred people in the place, a loud keening echoed. I scanned the ceilings and walls for something like a fire alarm that would be making such a racket, but nothing obvious caught my attention.

I felt more than sensed a wave of magic rush past our table as Jonathan sprinted across the room, cutting the music. "Everyone out!"

Whines and drunken protests went up immediately. The DJ even tried to turn back on the sound system, but Jonathan yanked the cords from the walls with one hand. Sparks crackled from the prongs as he caught the DJ by the front of the shirt. Jonathan hoisted the man off his feet, and I thought he was going to lob him over the turntable set up.

"I said get the fuck out!"

In all the time I'd known him, I'd never seen Jonathan kick the entire crowd out. This was serious. My stomach did a flip as I tried to process what was unfolding in front of me. After a moment of paralysis, I strode past Duncan and started shoving people toward the exit. I ignored the string of profanities the group of college girls spouted at me as I pushed them. "Come on, you heard the man."

The bouncer appeared in the doorway, blocking the crowd's egress and looking confused. "What the hell is going on? I've still got fifty people out here waiting to get in and now everyone's bailing?"

"Jonathan said everyone out," I shouted before heading back inside.

I passed Molly, Jacquie, and Duncan helping to disperse the rest of the crowd. I spotted Avery at the front of the pack leading people to safety. The keening sound continued, growing louder and more intense until it set my teeth on edge.

"What is that?"

"The wards," Jonathan answered. "Something's gotten past them and it's big."

"How can you tell?" Molly fell into step beside him.

A concussive boom echoed around us and chunks of ceiling began falling around us. Acrid smoke filled my nostrils, and I felt the rush of heat as something nearby caught fire.

EIGHT

We stood there as the keening finally died down. Or maybe the roar of the flames licking at the wooden surface of the bar and stools was enough to deafen the sound. I caught sight of a few stragglers in a booth on the far side of the dance floor. Smoke began to fill the confined space and I did my best to cover my mouth with my sleeve as I darted across the room.

"You need to get out. There's a fire," I shouted, gesturing to the burning behind me.

They stared at me glassy eyed and unresponsive.

Shit, they're paralyzed like stone.

I pivoted, catching Jonathan's attention through the billowing smoke. "Help me!" But the smoke and the crackling of burning wood ate my words.

I grabbed ahold of both patrons and hauled them to their feet by their forearms. I managed to drag them along with me toward the exit. I caught a whiff of fresh air as I reached the doorway. It was enough to clear my nose and lungs of the acrid smoke. I could hear wails of incoming sirens, but I couldn't leave Jonathan and Molly inside. I hadn't seen Duncan or Jacquie come out in the crowd either. I tried to scan the throng clustered on the sidewalk for familiar faces, but it was too dark.

Behind me, another boom shook the foundation. People screamed and ran in all directions. I pressed myself against the building to avoid being trampled as patrons and onlookers pushed past me in their bid to escape. The bouncer appeared in my peripheral and I spun to face him.

"There's people inside still," I shouted.

For all of his tough façade, the man looked terrified. He'd been working for Jonathan for a long time, but even that kind of time doesn't mean he was willing to risk his life to save his boss.

"I'll get them out," I said. "You just try to get everyone clear until the fire department gets here."

A little of his fear faded. He spun on his heel and began guiding people in a much more orderly fashion away from the building. I sucked in a few deep breaths of clean air before I darted back inside the bar.

Visibility had diminished to the point I could now barely see my hand in front of my face. I stopped before I got back to the bar proper. Running around in this mess was stupid and tried to center myself.

I had magic to keep me safe.

Trying not to choke on the smoke and ash, I called my magic to the surface. It wasn't as sluggish this time around. It bubbled up, eager to do my bidding. *Let me see and breathe.* Sparks flew overhead as the fire found the electrical systems in the ceiling. Chamomile blocked out some of the grit in my nostrils as my vision cleared to at least a foot in front of me. I took a step forward and stopped.

Why weren't the sprinklers on?

Jonathan might not always be the most law-abiding man and wasn't always prompt about getting his liquor license renewed. Though when it came to building codes, he was on his shit. He wouldn't operate without the appropriate fire suppression systems in place. They should have kicked on by now, given the amount of heat and flame engulfing the building around me. Yet the floor was dry.

"Molly! Jonathan!" I called out.

Crackling roared in my ears in response. My pulse quickened in my neck, echoing painfully in my ears as I took a few steps into the bar. Tables sat burning all along the periphery. The bar was a wall of bright orangey-yellow flame, and I could even make out hints of cobalt blue in spots where alcohol had been spilled in haste.

"Where are you?" I yelled again.

Even with my magic fueling my senses, the place was a mess. I wasn't fireproof and the longer I stayed inside the inferno, the better chance my magic would falter and leave me exposed. Déjà vu.

I moved in the direction I'd last seen the pair at the edge of the dance floor, but nothing stood out as bodies in the gloomy atmosphere. Above me something started to groan, and I looked up to see the support beams in the ceiling starting to give way.

Shit.

With a concussive 'snap' the beam dislodged and rained down ash and debris as it smashed into the floor. I threw myself to the ground and rolled out of the way toward the bar. Luckily, the very bottom hadn't been overtaken by fire yet. Out of the shadows, I swore I could see something emerging. I blinked as my magic faded in and out, and then I felt strong arms hoist me up from the floor.

Jonathan towered over me. "Where's Molly?" His voice barely registered over the noise around us.

I shook my head, fighting not to cough as the smoke nipped at the edge of my spell. "Haven't found her yet." He released his grip on me and started to turn back around. I snagged his wrist and yanked hard enough to get his attention. "We need to get out of here. Don't be a hero."

Before he could respond, another shape came at us from the opposite side of the space. As it grew closer it took on a distinct female outline. Molly appeared, hair matted to her head, face covered in soot. But she was alive.

"We need to get out of here before they turn on the hoses," she said between fits of coughing.

The nape of my neck was slick with sweat that I realized had nothing to do with the temperature of the fire. My magic flickered around me again. Sustaining it was getting harder to do. *Damn it.*

They needed me. I reached for Jonathan's beefy fist. I expected him to pull away, but he didn't. Instead, he slid his fingers between mine and held fast. "I'm going to try and extend the clean air I've got," I said.

I felt magic ripple up my arm as he gave me the support he could. I held out my other hand to Molly.

Her palm was gritty against mine as I envisioned my little bubble expanding further to protect them. Molly's coughing lessened and she was able to breathe again.

My vision blurred as we made our way toward the exit. Jonathan's hand dropped from mine, but I held fast to Molly. As the open door came into view, a high-pitched whistling filled the air around us. Whether it was a valve about to blow or something else compromised by the fire, I couldn't see. I just took off at a sprint, dragging Molly along with me.

A violent popping sound followed us out of the bar and something collided with my back, knocking me face first onto the sidewalk. I relinquished my grip on Molly's hand as I tried to brace myself. I only succeeded in scraping my palms against dirty pavement. A heavy rush of hot hair cascaded over my body as glass from the front doors shattered.

All around me, sirens blared and people shouted. The raucous became unintelligible as my adrenaline faded and the soot and grime caught up to me again. I sensed a presence standing over me and managed to look up into the face of a firefighter, mask already obscuring their face.

"Anyone else in there?" they asked.

"Don't think so," I coughed out as I fought to drag myself to my feet. Again.

The crew of firefighters rushed into the building with hoses and moments later I could hear the surge of water feeding through them from the nearby hydrants.

Finally able to get to my feet, I turned to look at the building as it burned. Despite the negative connotations associated with this place and my past, it still hurt to see it in flames.

"Kayla!" Duncan's voice rang out among the crowd, and I turned to find him racing toward me.

He wrapped me in a fierce embrace, so tight I could barely breathe. It sent me into another coughing fit, and he eased off a moment later. "Come on, you need to be checked over by the paramedics."

"Jacquie? Avery?" I rasped.

"They're fine. Helping with crowd control," he answered and steered me toward a line of ambulances.

"If you're not careful, someone might think you're trying to set some new world record," J.T.'s voice said from behind me.

I pivoted slowly to find him standing beside an empty gurney. "Believe me, I'm really not trying," I said, my chest tightening as it became more difficult to breathe.

He patted the gurney and helped me lay back. The gurney sat propped at an angle and the exertion sent me into a coughing fit. The world swam before me as my center of balance shifted. I sucked in the fresher air as I tried to fight back nausea and vertigo. J.T. positioned an oxygen mask over my face like he'd done yesterday and eased the gurney into the back of the ambulance.

"You can ride with us." I heard J.T. address Duncan as the sheer exhaustion of being nearly blown up twice in as many days caught up to me.

"Kayla, you need to stay awake," J.T. said from my right.

"I feel ... weird ..." I mumbled before everything went dark.

I COULDN'T QUITE pinpoint what roused me, but when I opened my eyes, I found myself in a private hospital room. I tried to sit all the way up and found myself tangled in wires and tubes. A bevy of machines hummed and clicked beside the bed, monitoring me. I turned to my left, toward the window, to find Duncan slumped over in a chair.

"Hey," I called, my throat sore.

He sat bolt upright at the sound of my voice and practically launched himself across the room in the same motion. "You passed out in the ambulance."

"Sorry ..." I replied. Swallowing only made the sandpaper feeling in my throat worse.

He handed me a cup of ice water with a straw and I sucked down some of the cool liquid. It soothed my vocal cords and I settled back against the pillows. "How long was I out?" The words were difficult and slow. Or maybe it was just the ache in my head that made it seem like they took an eternity to come from my mouth.

He checked his phone. "It's almost midnight. We got here maybe an hour and a half ago."

"Anyone hurt?"

"Can you forget for a second that you are working a case and just acknowledge the fact you nearly died ... Twice?"

"I swear I'm not doing it on purpose."

"As far as we can tell, there were no deaths. Some smoke inhalation and a couple of burns. But we got everyone out."

I took another few sips of water before managing

to push myself up onto pillows. It was only then I realized I was in a hospital gown. In a panic, I groped at my hip for my gun. We might have convened at a bar, but we were working at the time.

"My gun," I said, my voice ratcheting up an octave.

"Take a breath," Duncan said.

"Where's my gun and badge?"

He pointed to a bag on the table beside the chair he'd vacated. "All your stuff is there."

My heart thudded against my sternum in an erratic rhythm for a moment more before it finally settled down. "Did anyone see how the fire started?"

"Kayla, what did I just say about focusing on you?"

I waved off his concern. "Working makes me feel better."

"I didn't see much," he admitted. "I was more focused on Avery explaining what she'd found."

"Me, too." My ears began to ring and I flashed back to that keening sound—t he wards. "Whatever it was it had to be magic based. Jonathan told me that god-awful sound was his wards."

"I thought those were supposed to stop bad magic?"

"Not exactly. More like a warning, alerts him to

what's going on and he can decide what to do about it." I set the water down and rubbed at my temples. "I think whatever set off the fire was near the bar proper. I remember it coming from that part of the building."

"There's all kinds of things that could have set it off."

"Like a magic bomb."

"You think this is related?"

We'd have to wait until the scene was cleared before we could be sure. "It's as good a theory as any."

"If it was the same person, this feels like a massive escalation. The others were at least three days apart and done at times there weren't that many people who could be injured," Duncan pointed out.

"I know Notre Dame feels like it doesn't fit, but we still haven't found a connection between the other two scenes, either."

"Well, either way, it's going to be a mess in there for a while."

"Jonathan is going to be so pissed his place burned down."

"Damn right I am!" Jonathan's voice drew my attention.

He stood in the doorway, filling up the space just

like I expected he would. His clothes were filthy. He had soot streaks on his forearms and face, but he looked relatively unharmed.

"Shouldn't you be getting checked out, too?" I noted.

"Mr. Tough Guy here refused medical treatment," Jacquie said, squeezing in around him. She gave me a smirk. "Don't worry, J.T.'s agreed to give him the once over before he leaves."

"I didn't agree to that," Jonathan argued.

"If you don't want me to drag you to a bed and handcuff you to it to make sure you aren't going to keel over, you will." Molly's voice was clear and authoritative.

I couldn't see her behind Jonathan's hulking figure. But just hearing her voice eased the nerves that had been tightening my stomach into knots. It meant she was alive, and we'd all made it out. Jonathan and Jacquie each took a few more steps into the room and I stared at the empty hallway behind them.

Where'd she go?

"What are you looking at?" Molly's disembodied voice came from the direction of the doorway.

"Uh, not to sound alarmist, but is anyone else hearing this?" Duncan's voice came out strained.

"I'm hearing it, but I'm not seeing it," Jacquie said in a hushed tone.

Jonathan turned and his brow knit together. "How in the hell ..." He trailed off as he studied the empty space in front of him. With a determined look in his eyes, he waved a hand in front of him, like he was dispersing smoke. I felt the air pressure shift around me, making my ears pop. I winced, my eyes scrunching shut in an involuntary reflex. Between one blink and the next, Molly appeared. She was as grimy as the rest of us, but she had an aura around her. She looked just as confused as the rest of us.

What the actual fuck was going on?

NOVEMBER 17, 2019

NINE

"Can someone please tell me what is going on?" Molly demanded.

"Boss, you were invisible," Duncan said bluntly.

"No, I wasn't."

"Molly, you were," Jonathan confirmed.

This didn't make sense. The thrum of the machinery around me grew more pronounced and my head ached in time to the beeping and clicking. I turned my focus inward, trying to call up my magic to ease the pain.

Nothing happened.

I tried harder. *Kick this headache.* No scent of chamomile. No surge of energy through my body. I looked down at my hands, willing them to turn invisible against the coarse hospital blankets. Except the dirty pale flesh remained perfectly visible.

"Kayla, what's going on?" Jacquie's voice was soft.

I looked up through thick, unshed tears. "Something's wrong with my magic. I can't feel it anymore."

The room fell eerily silent at my words and in short order, Molly and Duncan had descended upon me. "Maybe you're just worn out from everything that's happened?" Duncan suggested.

I shook my head, the tears falling down my cheeks. "It's not exhaustion or the smoke. It's gone."

"I'd ask how that's possible, except we know it's been done before," Molly said.

Two years ago, the Order had stolen magic from the Authority's Council. They'd stripped magic from entire bloodlines. Ezri had been able to save some of them, but not all. I hadn't been involved in that case, but I remembered the turmoil the Order had caused.

"But I remember everything that happened tonight. Didn't the people who were attacked not have any memory of what happened?" I countered.

"I'm not saying it is the exact same situation," Molly replied.

Across the room, Jonathan stood, staring intently

at Molly. Her attention was on me, so she didn't notice. "What is it? What are you seeing?"

He turned his gaze to me. "She's got an aura and it's not fading."

"What does that mean?" Duncan interjected.

"No idea," Jonathan replied. "But there is definitely something off."

There were so many questions swirling in my brain as I lay there in the bed. Who could have taken my magic? Was this actually connected to the case? What does Jonathan know if it was in fact linked? And how had Molly turned invisible?

There were too many to try to answer at nearly twelve thirty in the morning. And just then, a nurse walked in, giving everyone, but me a disapproving glare. "Visiting hours are long over."

"They can stay," I said.

"You need to rest," she retorted.

"We could all use some sleep. We'll be back in a few hours," Jacquie said, forcibly grabbing Duncan's arm to guide him around the foot of the bed and toward the door. She eyed Jonathan. "You're going to see our mutual friend. I'll drive you."

Molly looped an arm through his and tugged him along. He didn't protest; instead, he followed silently behind Jacquie and Duncan. The nurse busied herself with checking my vitals.

"You know, I saw your chart. You were just here yesterday for similar injuries," she noted.

"Hazard of the job," I replied.

"Well this time, we're going to be keeping you for a bit. The doctor wants to monitor you and put in an order for something to help you sleep if you want it."

"Sure."

She nodded and wheeled the vitals machine out into the hallway before disappearing from view. She returned a few minutes later with a syringe that she inserted into the IV taped to my left hand. I tried to get comfortable amongst all of the wiring and waited for the drug to take effect. I could only hope for more clarity when I woke up.

THE NURSING STAFF must have checked on me in the early hours of the morning, but I had no recollection of their visits. When I did finally pull myself from the soothing lull of the sleep medication, I felt more alert and in less pain, than when I had since Friday afternoon.

I'd just managed to make a trip to the bathroom

when a sharp knock at the door signaled I had a visitor. A white coated doctor with a shaggy mop of dark brown curls walked in.

"Miss Rogers?"

"It's Agent."

"Forgive me. Maybe we should just go by first names?" he suggested. "I'm Simon."

"Kayla," I responded automatically before realizing he probably already knew that.

"How are you feeling, Kayla?"

"Better. Except I could use a shower."

"Glad to hear it. Could you tell me how you managed to get out of that building without any burns?"

"Just lucky I guess." In my mind's eye, I saw the ceiling beam come crashing down mere inches from where I'd stood. Apparently, the spell had worked as a buffer to keep from serious injury.

"It also wasn't the first fire you were found at recently. Anything I should know?"

I didn't like his tone. "I work for the FBI and on an active case. That's all I can say."

"I see." He studied something on the chart in his hands. "Well, while I'd love to keep you longer, I have a feeling you aren't going to stay put."

"I've got work to do."

"Do me a favor? When your case is done, check in with your primary care doctor. Just to be sure there's no lasting effects from your injuries."

"I can do that."

"Good. I'd like to see you get some more fluids in you and something to eat. And once you've had breakfast, I'll make sure you get discharged."

"Thanks."

He gave me a nod and turned on his heel, leaving me standing by the bed. I shivered as I remembered I wasn't wearing pants and went rummaging through the bag on the table. I pulled out the pants and coughed at the scent of smoke that clung to the fabric. No way I was wearing them.

"Knock, knock." Perris' voice drew my attention. She stood in the doorway with a change of clothes slung over her arm. "I leave you alone for five minutes and you get yourself caught in a fire … again."

"To be fair, I wasn't planning it," I said and hurried as quickly as the IV and wiring would let me to snatch the clothes from her outstretched arms.

"What's going on?"

I glanced at her as I tugged on the clean clothes. "Uh, we're working on what appears to be a serial arson case. Well, homemade magic bombs actually."

"You have all the fun, don't you?"

"It would be more fun if I had some idea of who was behind it or their motive."

"You've got a good team behind you. I'm sure you'll figure it out."

As she looked at me full of confidence, I couldn't help but grow teary. She was at my side in an instant, guiding me to a chair. "Did I say something?"

"No, it's just, things have gotten complicated. After the fire last night at Notre Dame, my magic is gone."

"Is that a thing?"

"Yes. I don't know how exactly, but after the first explosion two days ago, my power was shoddy ... intermittent at best. Now it's just vanished."

"Maybe it's a temporary side effect of the trauma?"

"I honestly don't know. And that's the part that scares me."

"I'm here for you. Whatever you need."

The door to the room swung inward and a nurse appeared carrying discharge paperwork. "Well if you don't mind, I could use a ride back to my place and then to FBI headquarters."

"You got it."

Ten minutes later, I followed Perri to her car in

the visitor lot. It was a mercifully short trip back to my apartment where I hopped in the shower and let the warm water cleanse away the grime and smell of the fire. When I emerged, Perri loitered in my living room, her phone pressed to one ear.

"I'll let her know."

"Who was that?" I prodded.

"Duncan. He's going to come by and grab you. He said there's a lead on the HVAC company. I assume you know what that means."

I grinned. "I do."

"Oh, before you go, I ought to return this," Perri said, holding out the extra key I'd given her. It explained the fresh clothes.

I waved her off. "Keep it. You never know when you might be back up this way."

She pocketed the key before we left the apartment behind. I found Duncan waiting in his car at the curb and climbed into the passenger seat.

"How are you doing?" he asked as he pulled into the flow of cars.

"I'd be better if people stop asking me that."

"Got it."

"Perri said you got a lead on the HVAC company."

"We did. Turns out the same one serviced both the restaurant and the massage parlor."

"You really think they're open on a Sunday?"

"I may have called the owner and advised it was in his best interest to meet us at their office."

"And what about Jacquie and Molly?"

Duncan fell silent for a long time. His knuckles grew paler as he clutched the steering wheel in a vice grip. "What aren't you telling me?"

"Molly turning invisible at the hospital isn't the only thing that's happened. She, uh, made something levitate after we left. J.T.'s been with her for the last couple hours and he thinks—"

"Just tell me."

"He thinks that she's somehow been given magic."

"But she's not magical," I pointed out.

He shrugged. "That's all I know. Look, once we pay the HVAC guy a visit, I promise we'll catch up with Molly and see what's going on. We're going to get to the bottom of everything."

The city passed by in a blur as I tried not to let my fears overtake me. I wanted to be optimistic like Duncan. But I'd seen what losing magic could do to people. It had completely reshaped their lives. A tiny voice in the back of my head taunted that I didn't even know how to be an FBI agent without magic.

"Kayla, we're here."

I took a few steadying breaths before climbing out of the car and following him up to a second-floor office in a nondescript area of the financial district. All of the other offices on the floor were dark. Sanders HVAC at the far end of the hall was the only one with its lights on.

Duncan knocked once on the door and it swung inward.

"Mr. Sanders?" he called.

A rotund man with a bald spot on the top of his head appeared. He lumbered toward us and pulled the door open more. "You want to tell me why I'm missing my granddaughter's gymnastics meet for this?"

"Because we're investigating a series of arsons and it appears your company did work at each of the locations not long before the incidents," I answered sharply.

"Oh ... Well, I'm sure that's just a coincidence."

"Did you pull the work orders for the two addresses I provided?" Duncan asked more neutrally.

"I've got them in the back."

We followed Sanders into a cramped office with just enough room for a desk, computer, and filing cabinet. He tugged the top drawer of the cabinet open and rifled through manila folders labeled by month and year.

"Ever think of digitizing this?" I muttered.

"No. I know exactly where everything is," he retorted and produced two order forms.

I noticed the same name on both forms: Michael Valencia. "What can you tell us about the guy who did the work?"

He took the form back and glanced at the name. "Mike? He's a good employee when he shows up. I've probably been too lenient with him on his attendance. But like I said when he's here, he's one of my best guys."

"You know why he's got problems showing up?" I pressed.

"His mom was pretty sick recently. He's been taking care of her and just had trouble getting in on time."

"We'll need his contact information," I said.

Sanders pulled open the lower cabinet drawer and rifled through the folder marked V. It was thin compared to some of the others. Not too many employees with last names at the end of the alphabet. He handed over a slim file labeled Valencia, Michael. It had a picture of his driver's license, home address, and phone number. It also listed his mother, Camile Valencia, as his emergency contact.

"Thank you for this," Duncan said.

"What can you tell us about the jobs he did at these two places?" I moved to block the man's egress from the office.

"Honestly, you'd have to talk to Mike about those details. I just coordinate the jobs. The guys on the ground handle the nitty gritty stuff."

"If we have any more questions, we'll be in touch." Duncan handed over his card. "And if you can think of anything, let us know."

"Sure."

I still didn't move. The fire last night had felt targeted. I hadn't asked Jonathan—and I hadn't confirmed with Duncan whether anyone else had asked—but it seemed likely there would be a work order in Sanders' file cabinet for Notre Dame.

"Before we go, I need you to check your system for one more address."

To his credit, Sanders, straightened and moved to the computer. I waited as the machine booted up and he logged into his system. I gave him the address. In my peripheral vision I caught Duncan's face as it dawned on him what I was looking for.

"Looks like we did some work there about two weeks ago." Sanders pushed himself out of the chair behind the desk and ambled back to the file cabinet.

He rifled through the files until he found the one he was looking for and handed it over. Sure enough, Michael Valencia was listed as the employee who did the work there.

"Mind if we make copies of these?" I held up the work orders.

"Knock yourself out."

I stepped out of the office into the larger reception area and made copies of the documents to take with us. I returned the originals to Sanders before leading the way out of the office.

"Good call on Notre Dame," Duncan said as we headed to the car.

"It felt like it had to be connected."

"Sounds like we need to pay Mr. Valencia a visit," Duncan said as both of our phones buzzed with the same incoming message from Jacquie to get back to headquarters.

Hunting down our HVAC technician would have to wait.

TEN

Seeing Jonathan sitting in one of the conference room chairs threw me as we walked in. Even in all the time he and Molly had been dating, I'd never seen them interact anywhere outside of Notre Dame. No late-night dinner pick ups at the office or early morning drop offs for that matter. He looked about as comfortable being there as I was having him present. J.T. sat opposite the bartender.

"How are you?" J.T. addressed me just as Duncan opened his mouth, probably to warn him off from asking the question.

"Confused. Pissed off."

"I would be, too," J.T. agreed.

"What's going on?" I turned to Molly. She sat in

the chair beside Jonathan, her hands not visible beneath the table.

"J.T. has a theory about what might have happened to your magic," Jacquie explained.

"But before I say anything, I need to confirm some details with you first, just to be sure," he added.

I slid into one of the empty chairs around the conference table and turned my attention to the paramedic. "I'm all ears."

"Okay, so you said you first noticed your magic was a little off kilter after the explosion downtown, right?"

"Yeah."

"And you noticed it was gone at the hospital last night?"

I glanced around the room at my colleagues. "I'm pretty sure any of them could have told you that."

"Jonathan mentioned he felt some sort of wave of power ripple from the bar right as you guys were getting out. Do you remember that?"

I closed my eyes, trying to picture the scene. I'd been focused on keeping my clean air spell going around all three of us. I hadn't noticed anything else hit me. Except the explosion that had thrown me to the ground. "I don't know. Maybe. I definitely remember an explosion of some kind."

"What were you doing right before it happened?"

"Trying to haul ass out of a burning building."

"You were holding my hand," Molly said quietly.

"His, too." I gestured to Jonathan.

The bartender shook his head. "You dropped mine before the magic hit. I wasn't near the entrance when it happened, but I think it knocked you square in the back."

"And what, you think that's what took my magic?"

"You said it yourself; you thought the bombs could be interfering with magic," Jacquie noted.

"That still doesn't explain what happened to my power and why it's gone."

'That's the thing, I don't believe it's gone," J.T. said. "I've interacted with your magic enough to be able to recognize it. I ran a few tests with Molly this morning and it's the same magical signature. Somehow, your magic has been transferred into her."

"But she's mundane." I looked at the other woman. "No offense."

"None taken." She tucked a few strands of blonde hair behind one ear. "But it makes sense. The things I've done so far are all things I've seen you do."

"As for why she ended up with it, I've had this

speculation that mundanes who spend enough time around magic can pick up on its use. And if they're open enough to it, might even be able to tap into the innate magic in the world," J.T. explained.

"Say that's all true and Molly now has my magic. How do I get it back?"

"I'm working on that. For now, I would say you should give her a crash course before she does something we can't explain away."

That suggested she'd done involuntary magic in front of people who weren't meant to know it existed. *Well, shit.* Heat crept up the nape of my neck and panic gripped my stomach, twisting it into nauseous knots. What did I know about teaching someone to use magic? Sure, I'd learned how to do it, but it had mostly been trial and error.

"I wouldn't know where to begin. Aren't you better equipped for this? I mean, you help train the Healer kids," I reminded him. "Not to mention, my magic got so twisted up it literally turned me invisible."

"I could explain the mechanics of how it feels to use my power, but Kayla, she's got your magic. You're the only one who knows what it feels like, how it reacts to emotional stress," J.T. replied. "I know this is bizarre and uncomfortable, but you're the only one who can do this."

"I'm a good student, I promise," Molly offered with a weak smile.

This wasn't the ideal place to train. There were too many distractions and I suspected neither of us needed our colleagues to pry, however well-meaning they might be. I looked over at J.T. and asked, "Do you think we could use some space at headquarters?"

"I don't see why not. I don't think the Council has anything going on today."

I turned to Molly. "We better get going then. Something tells me the time we thought we had between attacks has gone out the window."

"We'll dig into Michael Valencia," Duncan said, settling into one of the seats around the conference table.

"And we're waiting for Fire Investigations to confirm whether they found a similar device at Notre Dame," Jacquie added.

"When can I get back in there to assess the damage?" Jonathan sounded worn out.

"Once Fire Investigations clears it. But that could be a few hours yet, or maybe a day or two. You'd be better off going home and getting some rest," Jacquie answered, holding up a hand to keep him quiet. "Believe me, I understand that doing nothing isn't your default mode. But you need to let us do our jobs and handle the scene."

"She's right. We'll get to the bottom of this," Molly said and gave his hand a firm squeeze before standing up. She paused on the side of the table closest to the door and to J.T. she said, "You might want to come along. Uh, for research."

More like in case one of us got injured. I wouldn't say no to a little healer magic back-up. Time to see if I could actually teach my boss anything about magic.

WE STOOD in the Council chamber with about three feet between us. Molly dropped into a fighter's crouch. I just stood there trying to figure out what I was supposed to do and where I should start. Magic in combat was something that I'd always done out of pure instinct. It was all reactionary, but you didn't start there.

"I think you need to relax," I finally said.

She straightened. "You're the one who said we're on a time crunch. I figured it was best to jump to the defensive stuff."

"You won't be any good in a fight unless you can actually control the magic," I replied. "Tell me again what you've managed to do."

"Well, there was the incident where I turned invisible at the hospital. And I kind of levitated once."

"And what were you doing when those things happened?"

She rubbed at her forehead, brushing wisps of blonde hair out of her face. "I don't really remember. Nothing special. The first time, I was with Jonathan after he'd refused to get checked out by the nurses. And then, I was with J.T. and he was asking me questions about what happened."

"How were you feeling when those things happened?'

"Stressed. Confused."

"More emotional than usual?" I suggested.

"Yeah, I'd say so."

"Magic is tied to emotion. It feeds on that visceral need, whether it's to help or hurt or hide. Until you can tap into that with purpose, you're not going to be able to do shit with magic."

"Okay, so I have to get in touch with my emotions. I can do that," Molly said, shaking out her arms and bouncing on the balls of her feet. She closed her eyes, and I could see them moving behind their lids as she tried to concentrate. After about thirty seconds, she opened them again.

"I don't feel anything."

"Did you try?" I retorted in annoyance.

"Of course, I did," she answered.

"Okay, let's not jump down each other's throats," J.T. interjected. "Why don't you try taking a few deep breaths? I know for me, at least, that helps center me. It kind of opens up my connection to my magic."

Molly glanced my way. "What does it feel like when you do it?"

I'd spent so long trying to repress the power within me that even now, I could feel phantom ripples of magic cascading over my skin without warning. I shivered with a strange mixture of disgust and relief.

"It's kind of always there for me, right below the surface. I just have to look inward and it's there, waiting to do whatever I want."

"Deep breathing. Worth a try."

She took several breaths, her chest rising and falling in a steady rhythm. I strained, praying I'd somehow be able to sense the magic rising within her. All I got was my own anxiety ratcheting up my heartbeat.

"I can feel something is there, but it's like it doesn't want to respond."

"Both times you managed to do magic; it was a defense mechanism." I was grasping at straws here, but it seemed like a reasonable assessment. "Maybe we need to get you back in that headspace for you to connect with it."

"Well, I mean I'm feeling stressed about this whole situation. I don't like leaving Jacquie and Duncan without back-up, especially as we're dealing with magical bad guys. But I'm guessing that isn't what you want."

"No."

I surveyed the room around us and spotted several folding chairs that were typically assembled in a semi-circle when the Council met. An idea took shape in my mind. It was crude and J.T. would likely balk at it, but it was what I had. I marched over to the far side of the room and picked up one of the chairs. Without warning I spun like I was throwing a shot put and lobbed the chair in Molly's direction as hard as I could.

She gave a yelp and the chair sailed right through her, colliding with the doorframe on the other side of the room. I could barely make out the outline of her body as she remained translucent.

"What the hell was that?" Molly demanded.

"Not that I approve of violence, but it did work," J.T. commented. "Molly, look down."

She turned her attention to her barely visible state. "Oh ... I didn't even realize I'd done it."

"You had to have on some level intended that result," J.T. said in a clinically calm tone.

"He's right. Magic relies on intent, even when it's acting of its own accord. It has to draw a desire from somewhere. You knew you couldn't deflect the chair, so the next best option was to let it pass straight through you," I explained. "Good call by the way. It's what I would have done."

"I guess I did kind of have that split second thought. But is that really enough for magic to respond?"

"I'd say it is," J.T. noted. "But we should try a few more things just to be sure."

"Sure. But, uh ... how do I stop being all see through?"

"Just will it," I said. To be honest, I didn't know how else to explain it.

We waited there for a good three minutes until

finally she was back to being solid and corporeal again. "Uh, I think I'm going to need that chair."

J.T. scooped it up and unfolded it just in time for Molly to sink into it, head resting between her hands. "You could have warned me about the headaches." She took a breath. "You all make it look so easy."

"Magic always comes with a price, even if the toll gets smaller the more you build up your magical muscles," J.T. said. "Don't push yourself."

She gave a bitter laugh. "I don't have the luxury of waiting until I feel better. I need to get some semblance of control over these powers. Otherwise, what's the point?"

What was the point?

If the bomb at Notre Dame had been the cause of the magical transfer like we assumed, why even bother? Why give a mundane magical power? Most people didn't even know magic existed. And even if some random person found themselves with magical abilities, they wouldn't know how to use them.

That could cause a certain amount of chaos if the wrong person got dosed with magic. But that didn't seem to fit with attacking businesses. There were still too many unanswered questions in this case. We needed to track down Michael Valencia and see what he knew about the work done on all three buildings.

"We'll try something less intense for a while," I finally said when I realized both J.T. and Molly were watching me with expectant expressions.

"Like what?"

"Shielding conversations is useful. You just kind of project a bubble around the people you want protected and it muffles things for anyone outside the bubble," I explained.

"How's that going to help?" she muttered darkly.

"Coupled with keeping us invisible, it'd be really handy if we wanted to eavesdrop on potential suspects without them knowing we were there."

"Oh, yeah. That does make sense." She massaged the spot between her eyebrows. "I don't mean to come off as uninformed. I think it's just this headache is getting to me. It's like someone's got my head in a vice."

"You're here to help with injuries," I reminded J.T.

He stepped up and placed his hand on the nape of Molly's neck. The tension in her body melted away. "I'm not sure a two-pronged spell is necessarily less intense," J.T. commented when he pulled his hand away.

"We'll start with the easy part, projecting the invisibility. You already know what it feels like to be invisible. That's the one thing my magic is really damn good at."

"Start with extending it to one of us," J.T. said, taking a few steps back to make it clear he thought she should try to include me in her sphere of magical influence.

I watched Molly close her eyes and ball her hands into tight fists. I ached to tell her to just relax, that the magic flowed more naturally when a person was at ease. But she had to learn to control this in her own way. As I felt something wash over me, a pang of sorrow clutched at my chest so tightly all the air fled my lungs. I could still feel magic, but it was disconnected from me. It should have been coming from within me. I choked back that sense of loss as Molly's spell flickered and receded around us after about thirty seconds.

It was a start.

We practiced for the next hour. Each time, Molly was able to sustain the spell for longer and she'd even managed to sustain it around all three of us. By the end of the hour, she'd even managed to add in the muffling of our conversation. With any luck we'd be able to spy on Michael for at least five minutes before he noticed. We just had to track him down.

Molly's phone buzzed with an incoming text. My phone beeped, too. I tugged it free from my jacket pocket and checked the screen. There was a text from Jacquie to both Molly and I, letting us know they'd received new information from the forensics unit. They'd been able to pull usable fingerprints from the second scene. They matched Michael Valencia.

Maybe we were about to crack this case after all.

ELEVEN

Getting back to the office took an eternity. If I'd had my magic, I could have gotten us there so much faster. As it was, I was practically crawling out of my skin by the time we pulled into the parking lot. Molly sat behind the wheel, a pinched expression on her face.

"I know this has to be strange for you," she said as she cut the engine.

"You'd think someone who spent years having their magic control them would be happy for a little reprieve, but I never wanted it just gone."

"Well, maybe we'll get lucky and Michael will be able to tell us how to return it."

When we walked into the conference room, new information and images cluttered the whiteboard. I spotted a mug shot with Michael's name under it along with his date of birth and home address. He lived out in Roxbury.

"So, you're absolutely sure Michael was the one who planted the devices?" I looked to Jacquie.

"At the very least he handled the one at the therapist's office and massage parlor. Now that we've got prints identified we can check the other two devices for the same prints."

"What else do we know about this guy other than he's apparently a top-notch HVAC guy when he shows up to work?"

Duncan held up some printouts. "We confirmed his mother has been sick. She's got breast cancer and has been receiving treatment at Dana Farber."

That likely accounted for his missed days and late arrivals at work, especially if he was taking his mother to appointments. "Any other family we should know about?"

"Dad wasn't in the picture from what we could tell. And Michael doesn't have any siblings."

"So, it's been him and his mom most of his life. That could lead to him doing things that might be on the dangerous side if it meant protecting his mom."

"Cancer isn't a cheap disease to treat either,"

Molly interjected. "Do we have a sense of his financial situation?"

"From what we could tell, he rents an apartment in Roxbury not far from where his mother lives. He pays his rent on time. No outstanding student debt or anything like that," Duncan answered.

"Mom's situation is more dire," Jacquie added. "Like Molly said, her treatment isn't cheap. Even with insurance it looks like her credit is taking a hit, because she isn't able to make credit card and mortgage payments."

"Have we seen any unusually large deposits into Michael's accounts in the last few months?"

"Nothing out of the ordinary other than his paycheck every two weeks," Duncan noted.

"You're thinking he might be doing this for someone else." Molly looked at me.

"I mean it's possible, right? If he really wants to take care of his family, maybe he takes on a side hustle that pays better than his day job."

"But where's the money then?" Jacquie said.

"You noticed that his mom has a tanking credit score. Can we see her financials in more detail?"

"We'd need more than a hunch to go digging into her."

"So, let's go find something. We know where

Michael lives. We have a legitimate reason to talk to him."

"We don't want to spook him," Jacquie said.

I gestured to the mug shot on the board. "What did he do time for?"

"He had some drug offenses as a juvenile. Marijuana mostly. It appears he's been clean for the last four years or so."

Not the angle I'd been hoping for, but it might still prove useful. It seemed clear he was working with a partner to some unidentified end. Maybe Michael was just the mechanic building the devices. They weren't inherently magical after all. But we also couldn't rule out that he was the one setting the devices to blow.

"If someone is paying him, we need to find that trail." I looked over at Jacquie. "Do you think you can convince Avery to help us out one last time?"

"I'll see what I can do. And I've already got a judge working on a warrant to bring Michael in based on the new evidence."

In the meantime, we needed to pay Michael a visit and do a little extra-legal snooping while we were at it.

"We're going to go talk to Michael. See what we can shake loose."

"I DON'T KNOW that I'm ready for this," Molly said when we pulled up outside of Michael's apartment building. The sun was beginning its afternoon descent already.

"It won't be that hard. You only have to conceal yourself. Duncan and I will keep Michael busy. You just have to take a look around, see if there's anything obvious that will tell us who he's working with or what motivated the attacks in the first place."

She flashed me a small smile. "You have a lot more confidence in me than I have in myself right now."

"For what it's worth, I believe in you, too," Duncan offered from the backseat.

I turned to my friend and patted her arm. "Look, just focus on what you want to happen. Picture it in your head and that will help sustain the magic."

"I'll do my best."

"It's better you do it before we're inside the building," I said. I'd clocked a few police surveillance cameras on the street around us. We didn't need Michael's lawyer accusing us of shady business by having three agents walk into the building, but only two question Michael.

"But what about getting out of the car?" Molly sounded panicked.

"Remember that feeling you had when I threw the chair at you? Embrace that. You'll fade right through."

"You threw a chair at our boss?" Duncan said as he unbuckled his seatbelt.

"Just one," I said with a smirk.

Beside me, Molly's hands balled into fists again and her eyes scrunched shut. Slowly parts of her body faded until she was completely invisible.

"Good. Just stay focused. You can do this."

I waited for a count of ten then swiped my hand through the space she'd been sitting. I didn't get any sort of reaction, so I took that as confirmation she'd made it out of the car. Duncan and I left the car behind and entered the building, traipsing up three flights of stairs to the top floor. I could hear muffled conversations and dogs barking almost like ambient noise around us as we reached Michael's door.

"You still with us?" I whispered.

"I'm here," Molly's disembodied voice said from my right.

I knocked on the door. "Michael Valencia," I called.

My ears strained to hear any signs of life coming

from within the apartment. Nothing stood out. I stopped myself from telling Molly to take a peek. Passing through a car was relatively simple. It wasn't that thick. But doors and building walls were different. They were made to be sturdy. I didn't need her grasp on the magic slipping when she was only halfway through.

"He's got a car registered to him. I'll check out back and see if it's here," Duncan said, leaving Molly and I standing in the hall.

Beside me, Molly flickered into view. I caught the beads of perspiration along her hair line and her cheeks were flushed. She leaned against the wall, taking shallow breaths. I grabbed her by the elbow and led her back to the stairs, out of the sight of nosy neighbors.

"I think I owe you an apology," she said when she'd finally caught her breath.

"What for?"

"For pushing you to use your magic on other cases. I never realized just how much it took out of you."

"You get used to it. And remember, I've had it my entire life. Decades to learn to harness it. You've had, what a few hours? Give yourself a break."

"Even so, I'd be lying if I hadn't imagined what it

would be like to have powers. The fun I could have. And right now, I'm just hoping I don't completely tank the investigation."

"Yeah. Well, it's what makes me feel like I'm any good at this job at all. Right now, I'm feeling pretty exposed."

"I can guarantee you that you didn't finish top of your class at the academy, because you had magic. You put in the work to become an agent. You earned that on your talents, Kayla."

"Thanks. I appreciate you saying that."

She cleared her throat and pushed herself away from the wall. "Okay. Let's try one more time to see if he's home."

She shimmered out of existence again. It seemed to be a more fluid and seamless process this time around. We returned to the apartment and I knocked hard on the door. "Michael Valencia, FBI. I've got a few questions for you."

The door on the opposite side of the hallway opened and an older woman with wispy grey hair stuck her nose out. "What's all the shouting for?"

I pivoted enough to show her my badge. "FBI, Ma'am. Do you know Michael?"

She narrowed her gaze, as if to study the badge. She shuffled a little farther over the threshold of her doorway. "That boy is a good kid. But he's not home."

"Do you know where I might find him?" I caught myself before I let 'we' slip out.

"What's the FBI want with him?"

"Ma'am, please, if you know where I could find him, it would help a lot. I just need to talk to him. That's all."

"Today's Sunday."

"Last I checked," I retorted.

"He's at his mom's on Sundays. Goes over and brings her dinner."

"Thank you. That's really helpful. Have a good night."

I waited for her to close the door before I started down the corridor to the staircase. With any luck we'd catch Duncan before he headed back up. Out of the corner of my eye I caught Molly starting to lose her grip on the invisibility spell. Purely from instinct, I put my intent into the world that I needed her to stay unseen for just a few minutes more. Maybe it was my imagination, but the spot where I'd been able to see her hand a moment ago vanished entirely.

We found Duncan rounding the side of the building as we reached the car. I discreetly opened the back passenger door and gestured for Duncan to scoot in beside Molly. He did so without question. By the time I climbed behind the wheel, Molly had returned to visible and corporeal in the seat directly behind me.

"Well, his car isn't here," Duncan confirmed as I pulled out of the parking spot.

"He's at his mother's according to a neighbor. He brings her dinner every Sunday," I relayed.

From the back seat, I heard Molly's phone ping with an incoming alert. "Jacquie said the judge came through. We have both a warrant to search his home and as well as an arrest warrant."

I pulled to a stop before we'd even made it out of the parking lot. "If we've got the warrant to search here, why bother leaving? If he's actually with his mom, I'm pretty sure an hour isn't going to change things. Besides, it's not like he works on Sunday."

I caught Molly's reflection in the rearview mirror behind me. She held up her phone to show me a copy of the search warrant. "Let's do it."

There was no need for her to be invisible this time as I pulled back into the spot we'd just left. This time I marched up to the third floor and instead of heading for Michael's door, I approached the neighbor. I knocked sharply twice before the door swung inward.

"You again. What now?" She glanced past me to my colleagues. "I told you he's not home."

"You did. But it turns out we also have reason to see what's in his apartment. So, if you would be so kind as to tell me where I could find the building superintendent or someone with a set of spare keys, I'd really appreciate it," I explained with a sugary smile.

"Super's out of town, but Michael did give me a key in case of emergencies. Haven't had to use it until now though."

I held out my hand and mimed a 'give me' gesture. She let out a huff, but eased the door partway closed. I could hear the jangling of keys on a ring, and she finally passed me a silver metal key.

"Thank you."

"I hope he's not in trouble."

I didn't bother responding to her statement. Instead, I crossed the hall and unlocked the door. Thankfully, there was no deadbolt or chain to contend with. The door swung inward on silent hinges.

Even though we weren't expecting anyone to be there, protocol still dictated we clear the space before we began our search. I led the way, weapon drawn. I wasn't sure what I expected to find inside. But it wasn't a neat and tidy living room that flowed directly into a kitchenette. Everything appeared to have its place. There were no dirty dishes in the sink, no laundry—clean or otherwise—strewn about the place. This guy was fastidious. I found an organized pile of mail on the counter by the trash can. There were even little sticky notes labeling them as junk and bills. This was not the behavior of someone I would have associated with petty drug crime in his youth.

"Living room and kitchen are clear," I said.

Behind me, Molly and Duncan moved into the bathroom and bedroom, respectively. Molly emerged a moment later, holstering her weapon. "Bathroom is clear."

"Is it just me or does this kid seem like a neat freak?" I quipped.

"He certainly likes things to be in order. Everything in his medicine cabinet was labeled," Molly said.

"Doesn't it seem kind of odd that someone so organized and neat would leave behind physical evidence?"

"Bedroom's clear, but you two might want to get

in here," Duncan called out. There was a mixture of panic and excitement in his tone.

I holstered my weapon and let Molly take the lead. The bedroom was as neat as the rest of the apartment. Except I could see that the wall had been built out, probably unbeknownst and against his landlord's wishes to accommodate what appeared to be a small workspace. There was a cramped desk with a laptop sitting beneath the one window in the room, but I focused on where Duncan stood. The closet door sat open with a small work bench wedged into the built-out space. On the bench sat various metal scraps that looked eerily familiar. I even spotted a piece of printer paper with diagrams and instructions on how to assemble them.

"Well, if we didn't have enough before to bring him in for questioning, we sure as shit do now," I said.

"I'll get the forensic team down here," Molly said. "It's time for us to go have a nice long chat with Michael Valencia."

Camile Valencia, Michael's mother lived only a few blocks from her son. We waited until the forensic team had arrived on scene at his apartment before we headed out. I expected more news from Jacquie or Avery, but nothing came through. As we pulled into the driveway outside a row house, I pulled out my phone and dialed Jacquie's number, putting her on speaker.

"You have Michael yet?" Jacquie asked when she picked up.

"Just about to have a chat. Did you find anything else about his mom's financials?"

"No. Still trying to get access."

"Damn."

"I'm working as fast as I can here. Get Michael

in custody and that will at least give us a few days to dig deeper."

"We'll see what we can do on our end," I said and hung up.

"How do we want to play this?" Duncan asked from the front passenger seat.

"Jacquie still hasn't been able to get anything on the mom's financials yet. I doubt we'll get either of them to admit anything, so we're going to need to do a little snooping." I turned in my seat to face Molly. "We'll keep them preoccupied. Do what you can."

"I'll do my best."

I tucked the arrest warrant into my jacket. I'd been grateful to Duncan for suggesting we swing by the office and grab the copy from Jacquie. Even in this age of technology, some things still carried more weight in print. I waited until Molly disappeared from my peripheral vision before I knocked on the front door.

"Michael Valencia, FBI. Please open the door," I called.

Unlike at his apartment, the door swung open almost immediately and a frail woman stood before me. She wore a scarf around her head to hide the chemo-induced hair loss.

"Who are you? What do you want?" she

demanded, her voice carrying a strength I wouldn't have expected from someone who looked so worn out from treatment.

"Ms. Valencia, my name is Agent Kayla Rogers. This is my colleague, Agent Duncan. We need to speak to your son."

"Mom, what's going on?" Michael appeared in my line of sight about four feet behind his mother.

"Go back in the kitchen, Michael." She waved one hand in a dismissive gesture before turning back to me. "I want to know what this is about," his mother demanded, barring us entry into her home.

"Like my colleague said, we need to talk to your son," Duncan said in a calming tone. "Just a few questions."

I made eye contact with Michael over his mother's left shoulder. "We can chat outside if you would prefer."

"You said you're law enforcement? I want to see your badges," Ms. Valencia said.

"Of course." I held up my badge, letting her study it for as long as she wanted. Part of me wished she'd opened the door more, so that Molly could have gone in. Somehow, I caught the slight depression in the grass where Molly moved soundlessly toward the back of the house.

"Whatever you have to say, you can say it in front of my mom," Michael said, bravado in his tone. Either his mother knew more than we thought, or he assumed we didn't know anything. Neither option was going to make his day any better. "Mom, let them in."

His mother stood there in the doorway for a moment more before she shuffled back and opened the door wide enough for Duncan and me to come in. I positioned myself in the living room on the sofa facing the direction of the kitchen. Ms. Valencia sat in an overstuffed armchair and Duncan took the spot directly beside me. Michael hovered at his mother's side.

"Michael, you work with HVAC systems, right?" I began, trying to sound as innocuous as possible.

"Yeah. So?"

I pulled up in an image of the device we'd found beneath Dr. Abbott's office and held it out. "Can you tell me what this does?"

He studied it without taking my phone to get a closer look. Smart on his part to avoid leaving DNA or prints. "No idea."

"You sure you don't recognize it?" I pressed.

"Nope. No clue. I don't design systems or anything."

"That device was found at the site of an explosion a couple of days ago," Duncan jumped in.

"An explosion? What does that have to do with my son?" his mother interjected.

"It turns out that you serviced one of the businesses in the building. You also serviced two other buildings in the last few months where similar explosions occurred," I said.

"I don't know what that thing is or why anything exploded," he said. I could see his pulse quicken in the vein in his neck. He tightened his grip around the back of his mother's chair.

"See, I'm not sure I believe you, Michael. Our lab techs are really good and they found fingerprints on one of the devices. The prints belonged to you."

"No. That's enough. This is harassment," Ms. Valencia said, struggling to get out of her chair.

"You know what, I think this conversation might be better down at FBI headquarters. I don't want to upset your mother any more than we already have."

"You can't just take him. You don't have the right," she shouted.

I pulled the warrant free from my jacket. "Actually, we have every right. This is an arrest warrant for Michael in connection with these attacks." I passed it to her, but she didn't bother reading it.

Michael stood ramrod straight, one hand at his side, the other still firmly clutching the back of her chair. But I could see by the way he'd set his jaw; he knew what was coming. "Michael, please step away from the chair and put your hands behind your back," I instructed.

Michael did as he was told as his mother continued to struggle to get out of her chair, the warrant flailing around in her hand. I just hoped that by the time we got back to the car, Molly would have returned to her corporeal state and would be waiting for us. We didn't need to try and explain the appearance of a third agent in the house. As Duncan read Michael his rights, I scanned the front yard. My shoulders relaxed a touch when I spotted Molly sitting in the driver's seat.

WALKING Michael into the interrogation room without my magic felt like an even bigger test of my ability than just questioning him at his mother's home. My mind and body longed to try to see what was there, lurking beneath the surface. Without my power, I couldn't tell if he, too, possessed magic or if his mysterious benefactor was the one supplying the spells. And I couldn't just ask him that question without tipping our hand or making me sound insane in front of a mundane defense attorney.

"I told you I don't want a lawyer," he shouted when he'd been sitting in the room alone for ten minutes.

"Where are we?" I asked when Jacquie walked in. "Molly was able to find some recent bank statements at the mom's house before you arrested Michael. She'd been receiving large payments from a direct deposit account for the last six months."

"How much?"

"Two thousand every month."

"That's not enough to totally defray the costs of cancer treatments," I said.

"No, but it certainly helped put a dent in some of it." She showed me a printout of the account ledger. "Can we figure out whose account the money is coming from?"

"We're working on it, but the bank is being stubborn. And apparently, they aren't happy to be called in on a Sunday either."

"He doesn't want a lawyer," I said offhandedly.

"So, he's been shouting since you brought him in."

"No lawyer means we have an opening to ask about his connection to magic."

"I ran his name against the list we've got from the Authority and he's not on it. Doesn't mean he's not connected to it somehow, just means he's not on their radar officially."

"This guy is clean, organized. Part of me thinks he's got some sort of OCD. Doesn't seem the type to throw in with anarchist asshats."

"He could be a freelancer."

"Time to find out."

I straightened my blouse and led Jacquie into the room. Michael slid back against the hard back of the metal chair. "Finally."

"Something you want to get off your chest, Mr. Valencia?" Jacquie began.

"I don't have anything to hide."

"Are you sure about that?" I leaned in. "I saw how you reacted when I pointed out we had your printouts on one of these devices." I set the disassembled components of the device from the restaurant on the table between us. "You know you messed up."

"You're lying," he scoffed.

"We know you had a juvenile record. Your prints were on file with the local police," I countered. "So, explain to me, how your fingerprints got on a device that nearly blew up an entire building?"

"I don't know."

"Okay, how about you explain to me why these devices ended up at three of the jobs you did in the last two months?"

"Who says they were my jobs?"

I slid the copies of the work order forms across the table. "Your boss gave us these this morning. That's your name and signature on each of these orders. These three addresses all blew up in the last week."

"That's just some weird coincidence," he said in a strained tone.

"No. It is definitely not a coincidence," I countered. "This was planned and executed in a methodical manner. That sounds a lot like you, doesn't it? We've been to your place, Michael. We know you like things to be just so."

"You had no right to go into my home!"

"Federal judge said otherwise. You became a person of interest the moment we found your prints on that device. We found your little workshop, too. Sloppy, leaving materials out. But it makes me wonder, where's your next target?"

"I don't know what you're talking about." His voice jumped an octave, betraying his fear.

"We know about the monthly deposits into your mother's account, Michael," Jacquie said, jumping back into the interrogation. "Can you explain where that money is coming from?"

"You'd have to ask her," he said. The way he kneaded his hands together told me he immediately regretted putting his mother in the line of fire.

"See, we know that your mom has been battling breast cancer and you're a good son. You take her to chemo appointments; you cook her dinner once a week, so she has a nice meal. But that's a lot of pressure on a family," I said.

"She's strong. She's going to get through it."

"I don't doubt that. But I have to imagine that the bills are starting to pile up. Getting nice little infusions of cash every month must be something of a relief. Tell me, Michael, are you in charge of making sure those bills get paid?"

"What makes you say that?"

"Just a question. If I were responsible for taking care of a parent's bills, I would do everything I could to make sure they didn't have to worry about that especially when they're sick."

"She's been forgetting things. The chemo fog or

whatever. I try to help where I can. But it's always been just her and me."

"You're trying to take care of your family. I understand that," Jacquie said. "But the way you're going about it is putting people in danger. It's risking other families. That doesn't seem right to you, does it?'

"I think I want that lawyer now," he said.

"That's fine. Just one last thing," I said, catching the disapproving look on Jacquie's face. "How's your mom's magic been since the chemo?"

His jaw dropped. I didn't expect an answer, but it was enough to signal I was on the right track. This guy knew what I was talking about. There was no chance he would have gotten magic from his dad. It always passed through the maternal line.

"We'll get you that lawyer now," Jacquie said and stood up.

I gathered the evidence bags and gave Michael a last look. One last chance to tell me something I didn't already know. If he found a halfway decent lawyer, he'd give us whoever he was working with to make sure he got himself a lighter sentence. Maybe he could get out of prison before the cancer took his mother away from him for good.

He just slumped against the chair and turned his

attention to studying his hands. I left the interrogation room to find Jacquie waiting for me. Her look of disapproval hadn't disappeared yet.

"Look, I get it. He asked for a lawyer and questions should have stopped right then and there. But there's every chance he ends up with a mundane lawyer and I couldn't ask him later."

"It was a risky play."

"But now we know he's got magic. If we could just get him to use it, maybe we could see if it was the same magic that was in the bombs."

"Last I checked you weren't that sensitive to other people's magic, and you don't actually have a way to tell right now."

She wasn't wrong. And there wasn't time to try and teach Molly how to pick up on other magical signatures. From what I knew, it had taken Ezri a decade of hard work and practice to get as good as she became, and she had the added bonus of being the Savior. That lent itself to a power boost all on its own.

"We need to talk to Jonathan," I said.

"What, you want him to do a line up and pick out Michael?"

"No. But he could tell us why he needed to have an HVAC tech come out. If we can figure out the connection between the three places that were hit, maybe we don't need to go digging for magical signatures."

"I doubt we're going to get anyone to come down today. He'll have to wait in holding overnight. I'll get an agent to take him for processing."

"I'll grab Molly and we can go see Jonathan."

"No. You need to go home and rest. In the last seventy-two hours you've been nearly blown up twice and stuck in a hospital for long periods of time. I know you haven't gotten enough rest. Go home. That's an order."

"You're pulling rank on me?"

"Damn right I am. Not to keep beating a dead horse, but right now, you don't have the benefit of magical healing. You're just like the rest of us. And the longer we go without sleep, the more prone we are to make mistakes that can get people killed. So, go home and take the night."

I hated feeling like I was being benched, but I could see her point. As if on cue, my body began to ache from exhaustion and overexertion. Maybe a few hours' sleep would give me some idea of how we were going to get Michael to point us to the real mastermind.

NOVEMBER 18, 2019

THIRTEEN

I hated to admit it, but I did feel better when I woke the next morning. I lay in bed with my eyes closed. For a brief moment, it felt like my world had righted itself. I could swear I felt my magic itching beneath my skin to get out. But when I opened my eyes and sat up, reaching my fingers in a bid to summon my phone, nothing happened.

"Damn it."

I scooted across the bed and pulled the phone off the charger. The screen lit up with a series of texts from Duncan. I scrolled through them, kicking off the blankets as I went. He was on his way over and bringing breakfast. Via Jacquie, we then had instructions to interview Jonathan.

I'd just secured my holster and badge when a knock came at the door. I opened it and found Duncan standing with coffee and breakfast sandwiches in hand. "We can eat on the way," I said and moved past him.

"Good morning to you, too," he said with a smirk.

"Any word on if Michael was able to get a lawyer yet?" I took the sandwich and coffee from him once we were in the car.

"No word on that front."

It just meant we had more time to spend with Jonathan and try to fit together the disparate pieces of this bizarre jigsaw puzzle. I was so focused on my food I didn't realize where we were heading until we'd crossed into Somerville.

"Damn, I didn't know he lived out here."

"I've never seen that place empty, and I know they charge a cover. Plus, the drinks aren't cheap. The man probably brings in five figures a week easy."

Duncan followed the GPS in the car to a nice-looking single-story house with a driveway and a yard. I'd never pictured Jonathan as a house in the suburbs kind of guy. We were out of the car and halfway to the front door before I stopped walking and threw an arm to catch my partner.

"What are the odds that Molly is here?"

"I'd say probably fifty-fifty. Why?"

"Just not sure I'm ready to see that level of domestic bliss."

"She knows we've got to interview him. I'm sure it will be fine."

I lowered my arm, and we walked the rest of the way to the door side by side. I knocked once and then rang the doorbell. There was no response at first. Maybe he'd gone down to the police precinct, assuming we'd be there? I knocked again.

"Maybe he's not home," I said.

Duncan pointed to a front-facing window. A shade fluttered and thirty seconds later, the door opened just enough to show Jonathan's face. "What are you doing here?"

"We had some questions we needed to ask you about the bar," I answered.

"I'll come to you then."

"We're already here," Duncan said with a hopeful look.

"I don't really do visitors."

"Look if Molly's in there, it's fine," I said.

"She's not."

I gave him a wary look. "The longer we stand out

here, the less chance we've got to catch the bastard who nearly burned your place to the ground."

He let out a guttural growl. "Fine." He opened the door, and I was about to cross the threshold when I realized he wasn't wrapped in a glamor.

He had a large bony protrusion on his left shoulder that made it difficult for him to straighten to his full height. Out of the corner of my eye, I spotted Duncan staring, too. I knew this was why Jonathan kept up the glamor whenever he was at the bar. He could get by more easily with his handsome face and the strong drinks.

"So, what can you tell us about why you needed HVAC service?"

"The whole system crapped out on me, which seemed a little strange. I'd just had it installed brand new earlier this year. New ductwork, all that stuff. But I came in a couple weeks ago and it was just dead."

"So, you called for a repair?" I prompted.

"No, I did a fucking rain dance to fix it. Obviously, I called for a repair."

Duncan stepped up and showed him Michael's mug shot. "Was this the guy who came to do the work?"

"Might be."

"How'd you hear about the company?"

"They did work for me before a few years back. The owner was a decent enough guy."

"But they weren't the ones who did the new install?" I asked.

"No. That was the manufacturer."

"Did you notice the repair man putting anything in that shouldn't be there?"

"You mean did I notice him planting a God damn bomb in my bar and conveniently not tell me?" Jonathan was pacing the length of the sparsely furnished living room. "No. I didn't see anything like that. You really think if I had, I would have paid that little shit?"

I took out my own phone and held up a photo of Dr. Abbott. "Have you met this man before?" I flipped to a photo of the restaurant owner. "Or her?"

"No. Neither of them looks familiar. They're the other places that got hit, right?"

"How'd you ... right. Dating one of the lead agents on the case."

"Not that she tells me specifics. She knows better."

"You're sure you've never seen them in the bar as patrons?" Duncan pressed.

"You know how many people come through my

bar on a nightly basis? I don't keep track. It's possible, but you'd have to ask them."

"Is there any reason you can think of someone would want to target your bar?"

"You know I don't care who comes into my bar most of the time. So long as they aren't slinging around magic that can hurt people. But in the last few years, certain clientele have started to view me in a particular way."

"Leaning more toward the good guys?" I suggested.

"You could say that. Maybe I have. Does that make me a target? It could."

"Is there anything else you can remember about this guy?" Duncan held up Michael's picture again.

Jonathan rubbed at the stubble on his chin. "Now that you mention it, he set the wards off when he was working on the HVAC. I'd been recalibrating them, so I just assumed it was a false alarm. He wasn't doing anything that should have set them off."

Except setting a magically powered bomb.

"Thanks. That really helps."

"Right. Look, get this son-of-a-bitch before he hurts anyone else."

"That's the plan," I said.

We showed ourselves out and retreated to the

car. I downed the rest of my coffee while I waited for Duncan to start the engine.

"So, that was unexpected," he finally said.

"You didn't know he used a glamor all the time?"

"I guess I did, just wasn't prepared to see him without it."

"Hang on. That gives me an idea." I stowed my now-empty cup in the center console and ran back to the front door. I slammed my fist against the wood until Jonathan yanked it open.

"What now?"

"The day the HVAC guy set off the wards, did it have any effect on you?"

"What do you mean?"

"Could it have made you drop your glamor ... Even for just a minute?"

"Anything's possible. But honestly, you're lucky I remember him setting the wards off at all."

"I know. It's just, after the attack at Dr. Abbott's office, my magic glitched on me. It happened to Dr. Abbott, too. Could this guy have seen you without the glamor?"

"Like I said, it's possible."

"Okay. Thanks. Sorry to keep barging in. I'll see you around."

I sprinted back to the car. "I think Michael might have seen Jonathan without his glamor."

"I mean Jonathan's imposing as hell, especially if you aren't expecting it, but Michael was already setting the bomb. Wouldn't he have already had a motive?"

Something about this didn't fit right in my mind, but I couldn't pinpoint the problem. "Yeah, I guess you're right."

"He had a reason, though. If we want to find a connection, we should go back to our other victims."

"I think we should pay Dr. Abbott another visit."

DR. ABBOTT WAS FASTER to open the door than Jonathan, thankfully. And he looked almost relieved to see us.

"Is there any news?" He offered us water and pastries.

"We've got some leads, but that's where we need your help," I said, declining the offered food and drink.

"I'll do what I can."

"Have you ever been to Notre Dame?" Duncan asked.

"In Paris? No. I'm not much of a travel guy."

"The bar. It's down by Boston College. Caters to people like us from the community," I said.

"I've heard of it, but I'm not much of a social drinker. Or a drinker period. I don't think I've ever been there."

Duncan showed him a picture of the restaurant. "You ever eat here maybe?"

"Can't say that it looks familiar. I'm sorry, I feel like these aren't the answers you're looking for."

"We're looking for the truth," I assured him. "We do have a suspect in custody." I showed him Michael's picture. "Does this man look familiar?"

"I'm afraid not."

"You sure you haven't treated him before? He's part of the community. Grew up with a single mom. She's fallen on some hard times recently with cancer."

"No, sorry. I don't recognize him."

It was worth a try. "Is there anything else you can think of that might have made you a target?" I pressed.

He hung his head. "I know you asked me to look into any patients I thought might be capable. I'm ashamed to admit that I haven't done it, because I'm scared that it is someone I've treated and I missed something that could have prevented this."

"We're all human. We make mistakes and we miss things. That doesn't mean you've done anything wrong," Duncan said, patting the man's shoulder in sympathy.

"But if you could compile that list, it really would help us. We know that the devices are triggered by magic, and we think they might be designed to transfer magic from a practitioner to a mundane individual," I explained.

"That seems oddly specific. How did you figure that out?"

I took a deep breath. "Because it happened to me. There was another attack, at Notre Dame. My magic somehow ended up in one of the other agents. She's mundane. Although, she's been around enough magic over the last few years that she is sort of sensitive to it."

"Fascinating." His eyes lit up as if he'd just discovered the perfect topic for a research paper. I hated that look. "Did your magic return to full strength before this happened?"

"I think so. Has yours come back?"

"It has. It took until last night, but it's back to normal."

"We believe the devices are powered by the magic around them. The more magic that happens the faster they build up a charge and hit critical mass," Duncan said.

"We also think that the transfer of power might be the purpose. We just don't know why."

I could practically see the gears in Dr. Abbott's head turning as he processed the new information. "This sounds familiar. I can't put my finger on it just now, but let me do some digging. I'll send you anything I come up with along with that list of patients I owe you."

"We appreciate the help," I said.

I followed Duncan back to the car. I caught him watching me, an intensity to his expression. "What?"

"It has to be temporary. This whole no magic thing."

"I honestly hope so. But we can't count on it. Even if it is, it could be days or weeks from now before it come back. We don't have that much time."

"What makes you think that?"

"We don't know how many other places Michael could have worked. Or how many other devices are out there."

"I think we have a way to check," he said.

I stared at him, waiting for an explanation when

it hit me like a ton of bricks. Of course, we had a way to find out anywhere Michael had been in the last couple of months. But were a couple months far enough back?

"I know where you're going with this and it's a good idea. But we should make sure we know the timeframe we're working with."

"Short of Michael telling us, what do you suggest?"

"Have you checked to see if there were any similar explosions that hadn't made it on our radar?"

"I did, going back six months. Nothing else stood out."

That was a good sign. "Then we probably only need to go back two months."

Duncan dialed the number for Sanders HVAC and put the call on speaker. "Mr. Sanders, this Agent Duncan. We met yesterday."

"You the reason Mike isn't in today?"

"I'm afraid we are. We're going to need all of the work orders he's handled in the last two months."

"He is a good kid. Whatever you think he's mixed up in, you're wrong."

"We'll be by in thirty minutes for those work orders." Duncan ended the call.

"Does he seem overly invested in Michael to you?" I posed as Duncan revved the engine.

"Well, he did tell us multiple times he was one of the best techs he's got. And he did seem to go easy on him for missing work or running late. I don't know too many employers who would put up with that for six months."

I could definitely see Michael not calling his mother to ask her to get him a lawyer. That wasn't the kind of stress she needed right now. It didn't appear like he had too many friends on which to rely on. Maybe his boss was the person he'd turn to in a crisis. I didn't think that made Mr. Sanders complicit necessarily, but it was still something to take note of as we continued to dig into Michel's life.

We were halfway to Sanders HVAC when my phone rang with an incoming call from Jacquie. "Any update from Avery?" I asked as soon as I'd answered the call and set it to speaker.

"She's still digging. But Michael Valencia has gotten himself a lawyer and he's ready to talk."

"We're on our way to pick up some information from his employer that might prove useful now that he's willing to talk. We'll be back there in thirty minutes," I said.

"Make it twenty-five."

Duncan flipped on the siren before I'd ended the call and pressed down on the gas. I couldn't mask the excitement in my tone. I had a feeling things were starting to look up for this case. And maybe, just maybe, he'd tell me how the hell to get my magic back.

FOURTEEN

I tried to scan the information Mr. Sanders had given us on the way back to FBI headquarters. Except Duncan drove like a bat out of hell and I could barely string two words together. We passed a few police cruisers on our way. It was a small miracle that Duncan kept our own lights and sirens blaring the whole time otherwise I was certain we'd have been pulled over.

We entered our office to find both Jacquie and Molly waiting for us. "You're going to take the lead." Molly addressed me.

"Why me? You two have far more experience interrogating suspects."

"But you have a connection to him that I can't

fully understand, my current situation notwithstanding," Molly replied.

"He doesn't have to know you don't have your magic," Duncan said.

"I'll be in there to back you up," Jacquie added. "Come on. Let's nail this prick."

Duncan took the pages of work orders from me. "I'll see what I can find. Get on the phone with Avery and see if she recognizes any of the addresses."

"Thanks."

When we walked into the interrogation room, Michael straightened up, his hands still cuffed together through a loop in the table. I didn't recognize the lawyer. But with the way Jacquie reacted at the sight of him, I assumed he at the very least understood his client's supernatural pedigree.

"Well, we're happy you've changed your mind about speaking with us, Mr. Valencia," Jacquie said as she sat down.

"Before we do anything else, my client wants a deal. No jail time," the attorney said.

"Counselor, we have physical evidence tying your client to three separate attacks on local businesses. So far, he's got lucky. No one has been seriously injured or killed, but there isn't a jury in this city that wouldn't see our case and convict him," Jacquie answered coolly. "But if he is willing to give us details about who hired him, we'd be willing to put in a good word with the prosecutor and see about a reduced sentence."

"I was telling you the truth before. I don't know how my fingerprints got on that device," Michael said, apparently willing to speak now.

"Explain that to me?" I leaned forward, chin propped in my hands.

"I have to wear gloves when I'm doing repairs. No way for my prints to get on anything."

"Except we know you transported the device from your house. Are you telling me you used gloves to assemble them?"

His Adam's apple dipped in this throat as he swallowed hard, weighing what answer to give. "Yes, I wore gloves. I am not stupid. I knew it could link back to me if I wasn't careful."

"Let's put a pin in that for a minute, walk us through how this all worked. How'd you pick the targets?"

"I didn't. I'd get a text with an address and then a few days later, my boss would end up with a work order for that same address. He likes me, so I'd offer to take the job."

"So, then what? You just had the devices laying around in your little closet workshop?"

"No. Once I got a text with an address, that's when I made them."

"How many did you make?"

Michael's gaze darted toward his attorney who had gone silent the minute his client had started answering our questions. So much for advocating for his client or advising him to shut his mouth.

"I just did three." He voice shook, like he wasn't certain of his answer.

"Tell me where you put them?" I pressed. I needed him to confirm the locations we already knew about without being fed the information.

"There was a bar out near the colleges. The massage place downtown and there was a restaurant out near the Seaport."

"Your mother has been receiving deposits for the last six months. You and your partner have been planning this for a while."

"No one got hurt. Like you said."

"You got stupidly lucky," I snapped.

"How did you and your partner meet?" Jacquie's tone was calmer, more measured than mine.

"Around."

"Come on, Michael. You're going to need to give

us more than that. If you want us to tell the prosecutor that you're cooperating, you're going to need to give us a name. Otherwise, we're going to have to assume you planned and executed these attacks by yourself." I said, my voice rising in volume.

He pressed his lips into a thin line. He wasn't going to give us anything on his partner right now. *Damn it.* Time to change tactics.

"You don't want to give up your buddy, that's fine. How about you explain to me how the devices work?"

Michael slowly turned to his attorney who sat stone-faced beside him. "You want a lighter sentence; you have to give them something."

"It's powered by ... magic." He whispered the last word.

"We know," I responded bluntly. "Explain it to me. What is it meant to do?"

"It's just supposed to gather magical energy and then disperse it after it reaches a certain amount."

"Were you trying to take out magic? Is that it?"

"No. Look, I'm not the best with this stuff. My mom was way better before she got sick. It's supposed to channel the magic. That's all I know."

"You mean it's supposed to channel into someone," I pressed.

"I don't know." It was a lie.

"Are the effects permanent?"

"No way am I that powerful to make something last forever."

"Then why do the spell at all?" Jacquie interjected.

"I've changed my mind. I think I'm done talking."

I wanted to reach across the table and throttle him. The information we needed was right there in his head. If only I had my magic, there were so many ways I could have gotten it from him. I could have taken a stroll through his mind without him even noticing. Or I could have compelled him to answer. Now I was stuck sitting across from him as his attorney stood and waited for us to leave.

"You could have made your life so much easier, Michael. We're going to find your partner with or without your help," I said.

Jacquie trailed me as I left Michael sitting cuffed to the table. "Damn it," I spat and slammed my fist into the nearest wall. I immediately regretted the move as pain rippled through me. *God, I could really use my magic right about now.*

"We aren't out of options yet," Jacquie reminded me.

"You know he was lying to our faces. He knows so much more about whether this is temporary or not. He's got to know why those places were targets."

"You're right. But he's hedging his bets. It's clear he's loyal to whoever he's working with. We need to dig deeper into that and find that connection."

I nodded in understanding, trying and failing to ignore the ache in my hand. "This all just sucks, and I hate feeling this way," I groaned.

"You don't need magic to solve this case," she said.

I offered a bitter laugh. "Molly said the same thing. I'm not sure I believe it. Magic has always been such a big part of me. I feel so lost without it."

My phone buzzed with an incoming call, cutting the conversation short. Avery's name flashed on the screen. "Please tell me you've got good news."

"I think I found something. Can you meet me at Authority Headquarters?"

"I'll be right there." I ended the call and was halfway to the hallway when I caught Jacquie give me a half smile.

"See, things are already looking up. Go get 'em, Rookie."

THE CIRCULAR DRIVE outside of Authority Headquarters was packed when I arrived. I had to pull up onto the grass just to make my car fit. As I headed inside, I couldn't help wondering what had drawn so many people to the building on a Monday morning. Avery met me partway down the stairs leading to the second floor. She looked as if she was in a hurry. "Please tell me you don't have to rush off to your destiny right now," I said.

"No. I need more coffee."

I backtracked down to the first floor and joined her in the industrial kitchen. She busied herself pouring a cup of coffee into a travel mug and screwed the top on tight.

"What did you find?" I urged.

"So, Jacquie sent me over a laptop that your guys couldn't seem to crack. It was magically encrypted. Whoever this guy is, he's good. I mean ... we could have used him on our team."

"I doubt you'll want to liaise with a guy in prison for setting off magical bombs," I retorted.

"Yeah, no thanks. I'm just saying, his tech skills were pretty damn sophisticated."

It made me wonder if Michael had lied to us about his abilities and power level. "How much power would it take to sustain something like that?"

"I mean, not that much actually. You just need to be really clear with what the intent of your spell is. As long as it's connected to something tangible like a hard drive that has other safeguards like passwords and two-factor authentication, it's pretty self-sustaining."

My eyes glazed over as she talked. "Okay … uh, I only got some of that. Just show me what you found."

She led the way back upstairs to the tech hub and I found her screens filled with a bunch of open chat windows. I couldn't tell where she'd found them or what they meant though.

She took a swig of coffee from her mug before she launched into what she'd discovered. "So, our guy might be good at keeping people out of his computer, but he wasn't particularly smart about scrubbing his files. It looks like we've got messages between him and this other account, whiskeyand-wine23 dating back at least seven months."

Right before the payments started. "Please tell me they discuss money changing hands. Or any of the addresses that were attacked."

"A lot of it is about our guy's mom. It sounds like these two knew each other and not just in an online acquaintance kind of way. They talked about the old days, hanging out together. Getting pinched."

It sounded like Michael had a buddy who he'd gotten arrested with him in his youth. A new line of thought blossomed in my mind as I started to make connections. "J.T. had given us a current list of Authority members, but I'm guessing those names change as people move away or just stop coming, right?"

"Uh, probably."

"Can you look up records from maybe fifteen years ago? And run the last name Valencia?"

"Give me a minute."

Avery minimized several of the chat windows and flipped a cord from out of the laptop into her own machine. Her fingers flew over the keyboard so fast I wasn't even sure she was touching the keys.

"Looks like we've got one Valencia on the list. Well two, a mother and son."

"Let me guess, the son's name is Michael."

"Yes. So, your bomber does have ties to the community."

"Or at least he used to back in the day." I gestured to the laptop. "Did you find anything else?"

"Yeah, about six months ago, Michael mentioned that his mom was starting chemo and it was hell on their finances. His buddy, whiskey mentioned something about having an influx of cash and he'd be willing to help out if Michael could do a few jobs for him."

"Definitely sounds like they're setting up a partnership."

Overhead, something whirred and sputtered. Avery let out an irritated groan and glared at the ceiling. "Stupid thing has been crapping out on us all week even after they fixed it. You'd think people with magic would be able to install better ductwork."

"What's wrong with it?"

"No idea. I'm a techie, but I don't do that kind of tech." She turned back to the screens in front of her. "Anyway, Michael and our mystery chatter didn't talk much about the jobs. I think they were too smart to put that in writing. And if they knew each other in real life, it was probably easier for them to meet up in person."

"Michael told us he would get an address texted to him and then a couple days later, that same address would show up on a work order at his day job. That's how he knew when and where to plan the devices. There's nothing about setting up that system?"

"Nothing like that. Over the last few months, Michael did ask a couple of times why whiskey needed these jobs done, like he was surprised whiskey couldn't do it on their own."

That was interesting. It implied that our friend whiskey at the very least knew of the existence of magic. "How'd our mystery friend react to that?"

"Not well. There were a bunch of page long rants about how it was insensitive of Michael to even bring it up. There was a lot of anger in there too about how the world had robbed him of what was supposed to be his. He rambled on about how he was going to get it all back."

"Great, sounds like a lunatic."

"The communications stopped a couple days ago," Avery noted. "It looks like right before the explosion at the massage parlor."

"What? Why?"

"Michael sent a message a day or so before the first explosion, telling whiskey he worried that the work he'd done wasn't going to do what whiskey wanted. He said he could understand why whiskey wanted what he did, but that there had to be a better way to get it." After a beat, Avery added, "It looks like Michael wanted to quit."

It sounded as if Michael was trying to back out of whatever they'd cooked up together. But the devices had already been planted and it didn't appear he'd made any effort to go in again and remove them. I tapped my index finger against my bottom lip in thought. *Fingerprints.* Michael had insisted he'd been careful when handling the devices. He'd worn gloves at all times. But there had absolutely been a fingerprint found on one of the devices. And it led us right to Michael.

"You, okay?" Avery's voice pulled me out of my head.

"Yeah. I just realized I need to track something else down. This has been a big help, though." After a pause I said, "Did it seem like they had a falling out after Michael tried to end their deal?"

"Whiskey went radio silent after that. I guess you could interpret that as being a falling out."

It was worth looking into. If Michael knew his buddy had set him up, maybe that would loosen his lips more. Why protect the person who'd just thrown you under the bus?

"You said there'd been three attacks," she called as I started for the door.

"Yes." I didn't like where this was going.

"They talked about four jobs."

Shit.

At least I'd already had Duncan looking through the work orders. He was supposed to coordinate with

Avery. "Did Duncan send you over any other addresses to check out to see if they ping as magical?"

"Not yet. I've been in this guy's computer since yesterday and it's not like I farm this stuff out to anyone else."

She had a point. But it didn't stop me from being irritated about the fact there was only one of her. "Call if you find anything else. Thanks."

Given the frequency of the attacks, if we had a day before the next one hit, I'd be surprised. But we were still so far behind the eight ball. We needed answers and we needed them now before anyone else got hurt.

I made it downstairs just in time to see a young woman with a small child in tow, race through the front door. She looked familiar, but I couldn't quite place her at first.

"Alex, honey, why don't you go find the other kids?" she said, ushering the boy toward the kitchen.

He went without protest as his mother headed for the library where I only now noticed a sign reading, "Support Session In Progress." Our gazes met and she held my full attention as I tried to conjure a name from the recesses of my mind. The door to the library opened and Kevin appeared.

"Hey, Yvette, we're just about to get started." He spotted me. "Hey, Kay. Everything okay?"

"Yeah, sorry, I'm fine," I responded.

"You were a friend of Desmond's, right?" Yvette said, never looking away from me.

"I was. Yeah. You're one of the former Council members." It finally clicked in my head. Yvette and her son had been the first victims of a ploy by the Order to steal magic from practitioners and feed it to some creepy death monster. She was one of the few who'd permanently lost their power, even though they still had all of their memories of what having magic was like.

"I don't want to intrude, but would you mind if I sat in and listened for a few minutes?" I gestured to the door. "I think it could give me some perspective on something I'm working through."

Yvette smiled at me. "Sure. Everyone is welcome."

I followed her and Kevin into the room. I expected them to have moved the tables and to place the chairs in a circle or something, but people just sat scattered around the tables. I expected to see J.T., but he wasn't present. Maybe he had a shift or a day off. He deserved a day off.

"Hi everyone," Yvette began. She sat with her hands clasped in front of her on the table. "Before we start, I want to say thank you to everyone. I can't tell you how much it's meant to my family to have your support this last year. Losing my dad was hard, but I think we're finally in a place where we've found our new normal."

She wiped at her eyes as tears threatened to ruin her make-up. Kevin leaned in beside me and whispered, "Her dad passed away earlier this year from pancreatic cancer."

"Thanks."

"Anyway, enough of me talking. I want to hear how everyone else is doing." Yvette glanced in my direction. "Did you want to share?"

"Oh, no. Thanks though, I'm just hoping to hear from all of you. Learn how you're all coping after losing your magic."

"It's hard," she replied. "It's been a grieving process of its own. Some days I can feel almost like this is how my life's always been. But then I'll remember something or a smell will hit me, and it takes me back to when I had magic. It can be overwhelming, even now."

"You seem pretty well adjusted. There's no anger or resentment?"

"Why would we be resentful?" a balding man across the table interjected.

"You all lost your magic thanks to targeted attacks on your bloodlines. But some people got their magic back. That would piss me off, personally."

"I was angry, sure," the man replied. "But what's the point in being angry at things that don't exist anymore? Besides, we can't change the past."

He was a logical, rational human being. The person we were looking for had suffered loss and was still raging about it. They still wanted to go back and fix what was broken.

"So, you all feel this way?" I looked around the room and everyone nodded in agreement. "No one still gets angry about it?"

"We are here to offer support, not judgment. But in general, we do our best to focus on how to make our lives better with what we have," Yvette answered. The way her gaze dropped to her hands told me there was more she wasn't saying. But she wouldn't divulge whatever it was in front of an audience.

I pulled my phone from my pocket, faking an incoming call. "Sorry, I need to take this."

I stepped out of the library and paced the front hall, trying to decide my next move. Until we could identify Michael's internet benefactor, it felt like we were just barely treading water. I hated feeling useless. The door behind me opened and Yvette stepped out.

Her appearance had caught me off guard and I didn't have time to pretend to be on a call. "I don't know much about what you do," she began.

"I work for the FBI," I replied.

"Oh ..." She wrapped her arms tight around her torso in a defensive posture. "I don't know why you were asking if anyone was still holding on to their anger about losing their magic, but I thought you should know something."

"I'm listening."

"It wasn't just me and my son who lost our magic when I was attacked. My brother lost his, too."

"Anyone else in the family?"

She shook her head. "My mom passed away before Alex was born from a car accident. It had just been us and our dad since. But my brother, Jason, took it really hard. I mean, we all were in shock for a while. I tried to get him to come and see that we weren't alone, but he insisted it was too painful to be here surrounded by all these people who could still use their powers."

"You wouldn't happen to know a guy named Michael Valencia, do you?"

"God, I haven't heard that name in years. He and

Jason were friends in high school. They got into some trouble together, but I haven't seen or heard from Michael since they graduated. Why?"

The pieces were falling into place at lightning speed. "You said you lost your dad to pancreatic cancer earlier this year?" I asked.

"Yeah. It was awful."

"I can imagine. I don't mean to sound insensitive, but did he leave the two of you any money?"

"Why?"

Time to hedge my bets. "I don't know if you've heard on the news, but there've been a series of explosions around the city at different businesses. A restaurant in the Seaport, a therapist's office and a bar. They all had ties to magic. Michael is involved."

"Oh, God. And you think Jason might know where to find him?"

I stopped short of telling her we already had Michael in custody. "Maybe. I mean it's possible they kept in touch, right?"

"He might have. If I hear from him, I'll let you know."

"Thank you." I looked down at my phone as it rang a second time with an incoming call from Molly. "I really do need to take this."

I darted outside and answered. "Hey boss. I think I've got a name."

"That's funny, I was calling to tell you we think we might have found one, too."

"Jason Covington," I said.

"How'd you know?"

"Just had the luck to run into his sister at a support group meeting for people who'd lost their magic in that Order attack two years ago."

"Dr. Abbott came through and he passed along a handful of patients' names he thought might be a fit for what happened. He said that Jason was at the top of the list."

"Did he say why?"

"Said, he would explain to you in person. But I'm reaching out to Jonathan and our restaurant owner to see if the name rings any bells for them."

"We need to get Michael back in interrogation. I think I know how his fingerprints ended up on that bomb." There was silence on the other end. "Not long before the restaurant explosion, Michael reached out to his partner, to Jason I mean, and basically tried to quit. I think that pissed Jason off enough, somehow to go back in and plant a fingerprint."

"Any idea how he could have gotten the print?"

"If we're right and Jason is our mastermind, he and Michael go way back to their teenage years. They got busted for pot together. He probably had a ton of chances to grab a print then. Besides, it's not like it's hard to figure out how to lift a fingerprint. You can pretty much find how to do anything online if you search the right places."

"Duncan and I can handle that interview."

"Avery found their chat logs. There is a fourth target."

"Does she have any idea where?"

"She was still looking when I left." I paused halfway down the front stairs. "I can go back in the hub and see if she's found anything. Just tell me what you want me to do."

"She'll get in touch if and when she finds something. You need to talk to Abbott again and see what might motivate Jason to initiate these attacks."

THE TIRES SQUEALED as I pulled back into Dr. Abbott's driveway. He must have known I was coming. Since I didn't even have a chance to get to the front door before he'd opened it and was waving me inside.

"You ready to tell me what you know about Jason Covington?" I asked.

"I sent over the files I have here to your office, but I wanted to explain to you in person what happened."

I followed him into the house and he led me to the kitchen where he'd laid out some photocopied notes on the counter. "These are from some of our early sessions a couple years ago."

I skimmed the contents, struggling a little to make out the doctor's penmanship. The gist of it appeared to be that Jason was furious about the fact his family magic had been stolen and he was struggling to find a healthy way to deal with his emotions.

"I mean, in a way, I can't blame him. Having this piece of you that you thought was always going to be there just ripped out of you for seemingly no reason, it's a gut punch."

"Jason didn't deal well with the loss of his mother before then either. He came to me off and on during the aftermath of her death. When he came back after the attack, I'd hoped it would be with a fresh mind-set, ready to work on healing. But he just couldn't get past the injustice, the resentment he felt since some of the people whose magic was taken got it back."

"His sister told me as much earlier today. She

said she even tried to get him to go to the support group she helps run for other people who were affected, but it's like he's re-traumatized seeing everyone else who can still do magic."

"That tracks."

"Do you have any idea why Jason would target you? It sounds like you were trying to help him."

"Not long after his father passed away, he was spiraling into a pretty dark place. I tried to help him through it, I really did, but he just kept obsessing over what he'd lost. He needed to make someone pay for his suffering and when I wouldn't help give him a target, I ended our relationship."

"So, you cut him off when he needed someone." My words carried a hint of accusation.

"I could only do so much. I didn't think he was really a danger to himself or anyone else."

"He wanted to hurt people with magic. You know there's a whole community of people just like that. You didn't think it would be a good idea to give them a head's up?" I snapped.

"They were the people he was most angry with; however irrational we might see it. If I'd pointed him in their direction for guidance, I don't know what would have happened."

"So, he saw you as someone who was supposed

to be in a position to help heal him and you failed. I can see why he'd target you."

"If I could have gone back and done it differently, I would. But he didn't seem like a viable threat at the time."

"Did he ever talk about how he might try to fix his problems?"

"On a few occasions he did mention something about experimenting with some kind of power transfer. Something he said him and a friend had cooked up once while they were high." Realization dawned on him. "You think these attacks were to get power from other people?"

"It's as plausible as anything else." I drummed my fingers on the counter, looking at Abbott's session notes again. *Fingerprint.* "After the air conditioning system in the building was repaired a few months ago, did you notice anyone else come in to check on it?"

"No." He rubbed his chin. "But I do remember maybe a week ago the system wasn't on in the morning and the back door had been left open."

"No signs of forced entry?"

"Not that I noticed. My office seemed fine, so I didn't bother checking in with Marta. What, you think he snuck in?"

"Maybe."

Just then my phone pinged with an incoming call, this time from Jacquie. I gestured for Dr. Abbott to give me a minute and I stepped into the next room. "Yeah, Jacquie?"

"You still with the therapist?"

"I am. Why?"

"Because we've checked Jason's last known address and it's empty. Looks like he cleaned out in a hurry."

"Thanks for the info." I hung up and returned to the kitchen. "Can you think of anywhere Jason might go if he thinks he's being cornered?"

"You could check the cemetery. He told me that he would sometimes go there to talk to his parents. Well, more like rant. But that might make sense."

"No one else he'd turn to? What about his sister?"

"He and his sister weren't speaking last I knew. That could have changed, but I doubt it. From what I remember from our sessions, they were not in the same place emotionally on the subject of their father's passing or their lost magic."

"If anything else comes to mind, you let me know," I said.

"You have my word. But Agent Rogers, please ...

he's a troubled young man, but he still deserves a chance to get the help he needs. No one is served by him ending up in prison, or worse, in the ground."

"You've got a lot of sympathy for a man who nearly killed you."

"I don't believe people are inherently evil. They make choices that lead them down paths that cause harm, but they don't start out wanting to hurt others. Jason wasn't equipped to handle the obstacles life through at him. And as much as I hate to admit it, I wasn't prepared to help him deal with that trauma."

An unspoken sentiment hung between us. *Desmond could have helped him.* It was easy to think he could have done a better job when he was dead and people could place him on a pedestal. But I was beginning to think Jason was set on this destructive path and no one could convince him to deviate.

As I left Dr. Abbott's house to return to FBI headquarters, I couldn't shake the sense of foreboding. We still didn't have a location for Jason's final target. I just had to hope we uncovered his endgame before it was too late.

The office was a frenzy of activity when I returned. Molly and Duncan walked into the conference room moments before I did, and they were both deep in conversation.

"Any luck tracking down Jason?"

"Not yet. We've coordinated with local police to put uniforms outside of his building in case he comes back. But like I said, it appears he'd cleared out," Jacquie answered.

"We ran the theory by Michael that Jason could have planted the fingerprint as a way to get back at him for trying to break their deal. That seemed to loosen his lips," Molly explained. "He identified Jason by name and said that he paid Michael to set the devices."

"Did his sharing mood extend to our fourth target?"

"Not yet. But we think we know why he targeted the restaurant and Notre Dame," Duncan answered.

"Jonathan confirmed that Jason came to him looking for a job a couple of weeks ago. He'd been fired from his last job," Molly said.

"Let me guess, from a restaurant down at the Seaport."

"You got it."

"Even if they weren't rejecting him because of his magic, I'd bet that's how he perceived it. If everything for the last two years were wrapped up in this big change to his identity, any sort of rejection could trigger him. The therapist, Dr. Abbott told me that he ended the professional relationship with Jason a few months after his father died. If I were thinking like Jason, I'd see that as abandonment and I'd want to lash out, too."

"Any idea what he's after?" Jacquie leaned against the edge of the chair.

"The one thing he can't ever get back. Magic." I patted my chest. "Abbott told me that Jason and Michael once talked about a way to transfer magic from one person to another. He discounted it as being something invalid, because they were high when they dreamed it up. I think they figured out a way to harness the ambient magic around them and channel it, at least temporarily, into other people."

"But if Jason wanted to be there to absorb that power, how would he know where and when to be there?" Duncan interjected.

It was a good point and one I hadn't quite puzzled out yet. "I mean it sounds like he's not working, so he's got plenty of time on his hands. Maybe he is just going from one place to the next, seeing if anything had happened yet. We know from Michael that the devices were planted at different times, and we know that they each went off at different intervals. I'm guessing Jason had to have some sense of how long it would take for the power to build up enough."

"We didn't know to look for him in security footage before. But I'll get the guys on it right now." Duncan actually sounded excited by the prospect.

"Maybe I should try taking one last run at Michael?" I suggested. "See if I can get him to shake the information loose?"

"His attorney made it clear that Michael is done talking," Molly answered. "They're taking him to be processed since we've formally charged him with arson."

"They haven't left the building yet, though, right?"

"Kayla, he's not going to tell you anything," Molly called, but I was already racing for elevator.

I jammed my finger against the down button six or seven times before remembering that didn't in fact make the elevator come any faster. I didn't have the luxury to wait for the stupid thing to show up, so I shouldered my way through the door to the stairs and launched myself down three and four steps at a time until I reached the ground floor.

I burst through the doorway and sprinted out, spotting Michael in between two uniformed officers. His attorney trailed him, a phone in his hand. He clearly was through giving Michael any legal aid.

"Michael, wait," I called, trying not to pass out from the exertion of running the stairs.

He stopped walking and the guards on either side of him stopped, too. It gave me enough time to catch up and position myself in front of them. "Give me a minute, guys."

They didn't like the idea of leaving their charge unattended. But I showed them my badge and they took a few steps away. I could have used Molly casting a spell to muffle our conversation, but no such luck.

"I need to know one thing. I promise, just answer this one question and I will leave you alone."

Michael glanced over his shoulder at his attorney who wasn't even paying attention. What an asshole. "I already told the other agents everything I'm going to say."

"You already gave us Jason, because he pinned this on you. But you're still keeping things secret. When we last saw each other, you told me you'd only made three devices. We know there's one more location.. Just pointing the finger back at Jason isn't going to be enough to get you leniency. So, stop lying to me and help yourself here, Michael."

"I thought you had a question," he quipped.

"Why did you leave the Authority?"

Surprise colored his cheeks. "Mom got fed up with them. She thought they were a bunch of elitist pricks. She wasn't wrong, either. She only stayed as long as she did, because my grandmother thought they all walked on water. After she died, Mom bailed."

"So, you don't have any love for them either?" A knot formed in my stomach, bringing with it flashes of heat and nausea. I was beginning to suspect I knew where to look for Jason's final target.

"That's two questions. I'm done talking."

"Good luck in prison, Michael. Say hi to Jamison Taggart for me. You two might actually get along." I waved for the other officers to retake custody of him as I made my way back upstairs. The entire way up, I obsessively checked my phone for any missed messages from Avery or maybe even Yvette.

Nothing.

When I got back upstairs, Duncan had laid out all of Michael's work orders for the last two months on the whiteboard and was on the phone with Avery —I could hear her voice on speakerphone—as they ran through them one by one. I walked up and studied the latest ones. The most recent job was the day before the explosion at Dr. Abbott's. The address looked so familiar. But I was terrible with visualizing geography without reference points.

"The last one. Get it on a map. Now," I told Duncan.

"Give me a minute."

He pulled it up on his computer and turned it so I could see the screen. The image on the map was all I needed to confirm my suspicions. My stomach did a series of flips.

"Avery, what exactly do you know about the work that was done at Headquarters last week?"

"You mean the heating system? Just that we had

to make sure we cleared most of the meetings out when the guy came. I wasn't actually here when they were doing the work. But I think J.T. was."

"How many people are there right now?"

"Fifty. Maybe sixty. Why?"

"You need to get them out of there now."

"What am I supposed to tell them?"

"Anything. Whatever you have to in order to get them away from the building. Avery, please just do it."

I pulled out my phone and texted J.T. an image of Michael's mug shot with a question about whether he recognized him from the HVAC work done the prior week. J.T. replied almost immediately in the affirmative.

"We know his next target," I said and jabbed my finger at the work order. "It all makes sense. Jason hated the Authority. It represented everything he lost and could no longer have."

"And it would be somewhere he knew magic would build up quickly. I wouldn't be surprised if he went by and intentionally broke something to ensure they had to call for repairs," Duncan offered.

"Michael probably had business cards on him. It wouldn't be difficult for Jason to take a few and leave them, so that whoever discovered the broken system would reach out," Jacquie added.

"We need to get over there now," I insisted and led the way back to the parking lot. "I also know why Michael kept his mouth shut about the last target. He didn't like the Authority either. I think in a way, it's personal for him, too."

We piled into an SUV and headed out. On the way, I listened as Jacquie called in back-up and fire rescue teams to be on standby. I hoped we wouldn't need them, but it was better to be prepared.

"I just got confirmation from our techs. They were able to find Jason outside the restaurant on at least three different occasions leading up to the explosion. I don't think he expected it to happen in the morning, because he wasn't there at the time of the explosion."

"What about the other two?"

"They're still looking. But it would have been really easy for him to blend in with the lines waiting to get into Notre Dame. He wouldn't even have to go in. You were out of the building when your magic took the hit."

"He probably thought if the bar went up, Jonathan would be the last person out and he could get close enough for his magic to transfer," I said.

Jacquie pressed down on the gas and flipped the sirens on as we found ourselves in the heavy flow of traffic leaving the city for the day. As we wove through vehicles on the highway, my phone buzzed with an unknown number.

"Agent Rogers," I answered.

"Kayla, it's Yvette. J.T. gave me your number." I picked up on the panic in her voice.

"What's going on?"

"Jason called. He wanted to know where I was. He told me that I should take Alex and get away from Authority Headquarters for a while. He didn't sound well." I could hear the emotion in her voice as she fought to keep from breaking down. "My brother's involved in this, too, isn't he?"

"You need to get away from the building. Take Alex and get as far as you can. It isn't safe," I replied.

"Is this my fault?" she sniffled.

"None of this is your fault. It's not anyone's fault," I answered, trying to distract her. I hit the mute button on my phone. To Jacquie I said. "I think he's already there. He called his sister and warned her to get clear. I think he knows this is going to get bad and he doesn't want the one person he still has a connection with to get hurt."

"Hello? Kayla are you there?" Yvette's voice hitched on the other end of the line.

I unmuted myself. "I'm here. Just get your son and go. We're going to do everything we can to bring Jason in quietly and peacefully."

It was all I could promise her now. It was really up to Jason what happened next. I just hoped he wasn't too far gone.

SEVENTEEN

Where the circular drive had been crammed full of cars only an hour ago, there now sat a single car parked at the far edge of the drive. I recognized it as Avery's. Damn it. If she got herself hurt or killed, Des would come back from beyond the grave and give me shit until the end of time.

I was out of the car before Jacquie had a chance to put it in park. At least I had enough sense to put on my tactical vest before leaving the vehicle behind me. Though it wasn't going to do much for me if I got blown up, but it was better than nothing. My gun was drawn as I approached the front steps. I heard movement from beyond the partially opened door, and I led with the muzzle of my weapon. Someone shrieked as I grabbed a fistful of shirt.

I pulled Avery from behind the door, her glasses askew as she held her hands up to avoid getting shot. "Fuck. I thought I told you to get everyone out."

"I did. I've been trying to determine where the device was placed."

I hauled Avery onto the front steps. "That's our job."

"This is a big building and it got me thinking, why use one device when you could use multiple. Twice the power boost."

"Great. We'll take it from here."

"There's a utility room in the basement and most of the ductwork runs through the Council meeting chamber."

By this point, Jacquie, Molly, and Duncan had joined us. "We appreciate the information, but Kayla is right. You need to get out of here," Molly insisted.

"But I can help," Avery protested.

"You told me you've got a bigger destiny coming for you. It's pretty damn hard to meet it if you're dead," Jacquie noted.

"Okay. I get it. Just remember, basement and—"

"Council chamber." I cut her off.

Duncan took Avery by the wrist and guided her back behind the safety of our SUV. In the distance I picked up on sirens coming our way. If Jason didn't know we were here, he would now.

"What exactly is our plan?" Molly hissed with her weapon drawn, but pointed toward the ground at her side.

I had been winging it. Part of me had hoped I could simply talk Jason down and convince him to cut the bomb's proverbial power source. As we stood outside of the building that symbolized everything that had gone to shit in his life, I realized that wasn't a viable option. Even if Jason had wanted to defuse the devices, he didn't have magic.

"We split up, but stay on comms," I finally said. "If Avery is right, you'll find a device in the basement."

"And what exactly am I supposed to do with it? In case you missed it, I am not a bomb disposal tech."

"It should actually be easier than disarming a regular bomb," I answered with a hint of hope in my voice. "You just have to redirect the intent of the spell."

"You talk like that's easy."

"I'm starting to think this wasn't random chance that you ended up with my magic. You are incredibly calm under pressure, and you have a reverence for the power I've only ever seen in people born with magic. You can do this."

Without responding, Molly charged through the front door with her weapon ready. The rest of us followed after her. Jacquie and Duncan headed for the back of the building while I secured the first floor.

"Kitchen's clear," Jacquie's voice said in my ear.

I moved through the library, but found no evidence that Jason was waiting in there for us. "Library is clear."

"Basement is clear, but Avery was right. There is a device down here," Molly's voice said in my ear. It carried a strained quality that worried me.

"What's wrong?"

"It feels like all the air in the room is pressing down on me, like I can't breathe," she replied.

"The magic is building up. It's going to detonate soon."

"Stay calm," Molly said aloud.

"Okay, do you see any way to disengage it from the rest of the system?"

"I'm looking." The silence that followed over the comms was deafening. I moved out of the library and approached the stairs that led up to the second floor.

"Did you find anything?" Duncan's voice broke the silence.

"It doesn't look like I can free it. What do I do with it?"

"You can feel the power coming off of it right?"

"Painfully so."

"You need to push back against the spell. Instead of letting it build, you need to just send it out into the world."

"Won't that just make it blow up?"

"You're overriding the magic. Giving it a new purpose." If she couldn't do it, I needed to at least try to find Jason and dismantle the second device.

I crept up the stairs, weapon still drawn as I approached the Council chamber. My shoes squeaked on the flooring as I nudged the door open with my foot and darted inside. Jason stood by the window, his back to me. I could see where the second device protruded from exposed ceiling panels. It might have been my brain filling in the gaps based on what Molly had told me, but I could swear the air felt heavier here, too. Very much like it had right before Dr. Abbott's office exploded.

"It's over Jason," I called.

He turned slowly to face me. "Not yet. But soon it will be."

"You think that this is going to give you power?" I said, weapon still trained on him.

"I know it will." He pointed to me. "I was there. I know it happened to you."

"You're right, it did. I lost my magic. But it was only temporary," I bluffed.

"You're lying. I know it's gone."

"You can't just rip someone else's magic out of them. Don't you see that you're doing the same thing that was done to you?"

"No. I'm not taking people's magic. It's victimless. Magic is everywhere. It wants to be used; no, it *needs* to be used. I'm just giving it a conduit to act through."

"I understand why you'd want it back," I said, lowering my gun. "Being without it even for just a little while, it's felt like a piece of me was missing. Like suddenly I was walking around without an arm. But lashing out like this isn't going to make things better."

"It doesn't matter. In a few minutes I'll have everything I need."

"If that were true and you think this is victimless, why tell your sister and nephew to steer clear? They were hurt just like you. Don't they deserve some of the power?"

"They gave up."

"Why, because they moved on with their lives? I saw your sister today. It's still a struggle for her every day to get up and move forward. But that's what she has to do. She can't live in the past, Jason. And neither can you."

"I think I managed to reverse the bomb. It feels a lot lighter in here now," Molly said in my earpiece.

The moment she spoke, something shifted around me. The weight I thought I'd sensed before became agonizingly real. I felt like I was swimming through sludge. I glanced down at my hand and sent out the tiny thought that it would be great if right now he couldn't see my left hand. It disappeared up to the wrist.

How did that happen?

"Jason, look at me. You need to disarm this device before anyone else gets hurt," I argued, gesturing to the device overhead. "We've got Michael in custody. We know you were paying him to help you. And we know you snuck back in and planted evidence to frame him after he tried to back out."

"It isn't fair," he spat. "I can't make the people who took it from me pay. They don't even know magic exists anymore. And can't make the people who failed to give it back understand what it feels like, because they're all dead."

"So, you're lashing out at the people around you, the ones you think abandoned you. I can guarantee that none of them turned on you, because you don't have magic anymore."

The energy around me continued to grow. This needed to end now. If I could get Jason out of the mix, then maybe I had a shot of disarming the device before the whole building came down around us. I heard footsteps on the stairs outside and wished I had a good way to warn off the calvary.

"Jason, I don't think you wanted innocent people to get hurt, did you?"

"What?"

"You planned these devices to go off when there weren't that many people around. You've gotten lucky so far. No one has been seriously injured or killed. If you don't help me disarm this device and four federal agents die as a result, there's going to be no hope for your future. They'll put you on death row. I don't want to see that happen to you."

"It isn't fair ..." he repeated, as if he hadn't heard me.

The air around me made my ears pop and my teeth ache. I was running out of time. He began to pace back and forth, just rambling to himself about the inequity of his situation. It was the opening I needed. I rushed Jason and tackled him to the ground. I flipped him onto his stomach and pinning him down with my knee in the small of his back. I secured his hands behind him in cuffs.

The door to my left burst open and Jacquie appeared. "You need to get him the hell out of here," I said as I hauled Jason to his feet.

"Something happened in the basement. After she confirmed she'd diverted the device, Molly passed out."

"Maybe it was Michael's original spell coming to the natural end of its existence. Or maybe somehow redirecting the energy reset the balance of things, but my magic is back where it belongs." I shoved Jason into her arms. "Not that it's going to matter if I can't disarm this damn thing in the next couple of minutes."

I dragged a chair over to stand beneath the device. I could see it was secured with metal brackets that weren't really meant to fit on the ducts running through the ceiling. I reached into the small space between the duct and surrounding ceiling to see if I could locate any weak points. The brackets only went about halfway around the pipe. Except when I tried to dig my hands in around the device, it wouldn't budge.

Time to see if my magic really was back in action.

Disconnect this from the pipe.

Slowly, I could hear metal shearing as the bolts pried themselves loose. The Authority might need another repair job after this, but at least they wouldn't have a building to repair. My arms grew heavy as I set the device on the floor.

"Okay, you can do this Kayla."

Return the energy to where it came from.

The air around me only grew heavier, more cloying. Either I'd put the wrong intent out into the world, or my magic wasn't back to full strength. Either way, I saw only one way forward.

Please, please let this not be a stupid idea.

The pressure around me became suffocating as the device prepared to detonate. I threw myself on top of it, curled into as tight a ball as I could, and waited. The shockwave rippled over me, and I thought every bone in my body was about to be crushed from the weight. My nerves tingled and my eyes burned, but I was still very much alive. The scent of chamomile coated my tongue and throat. It felt like I was drenched in tea as the energy dissipated around me. The world flickered in and out of focus as my heart hammered so hard in my ears that I thought I'd go deaf from the sound. But it meant I was still alive. I'd done it. Somehow, I'd actually saved the day.

NOVEMBER 30, 2019

EIGHTEEN

It still didn't feel real that it had been nearly two weeks since we'd averted the Authority Headquarters from being blown sky high. Jason Covington and Michael Valencia now sat behind bars awaiting trial. If they were both smart, they'd accept whatever plea deals the prosecution offered. It would make everyone's lives much easier in the long run. Especially for us, we wouldn't have to find creative ways to explain Jason's true motives behind the attacks.

When I'd started this case, I couldn't have imagined I would have really understood our suspect's motivations. But spending even a couple of days without my magic had allowed me to see what Jason's life had been like for the last two years. He hadn't done anything to anyone and yet he'd been unceremoniously stripped of his family's birthright. I'd hated the feeling of jealousy that had bubbled to the surface as I watched Molly try to wrangle power that wasn't meant for her. To see that she had something that rightfully belonged to me, however temporary. In a way, I couldn't blame Jason for lashing out. However, that didn't mean the way he'd done it was right.

"You're awfully quiet," Perri said from the passenger seat.

I shook the mental cobwebs from my mind and turned my attention to my friend. She'd ended up staying in Boston through the holidays and I'd agreed to take her to Logan Airport, so she could catch her flight back to D.C.

"Sorry, just thinking about everything that happened on this case."

"It's okay. It's a lot to wrap your head around."

"There were a few times where I didn't think things were going to break our way. We almost didn't get to the Authority Headquarters in time to stop Jason."

"But you did. And you got your magic back. Everything is as it's supposed to be."

Well, not everything.

"You're right. We averted disaster and I know

I've got people who have my back, magic or not. It's not a place I thought I'd ever be. But it's one I'm going to hold on to for as long as I can."

"You better. Because before you know it, I'll be back and you'll have me in your corner, too, Kay."

"Thanks."

"And there's your very sweet, devoted partner to keep you cozy in the meantime," she said with a laugh.

I almost let out a groan in response. Not because I didn't relish the idea of cozying up to Duncan on a couch somewhere, but because I should have expected her parting words to be about my love life.

"I promise, if anything more develops there, you'll be the first one I tell," I said.

She winked at me. "Hope I don't know before he does."

A loud horn blared behind us, and I realized we were blocking drop off traffic at the terminal. I resisted the urge to flip off the driver behind us and gave Perri an embrace before she left the car, suitcase rolling next to her.

The car behind me continued honking. I rolled my eyes as I pulled away from the curb and left the airport behind. As I made it to the tunnel that would take me downtown again, my phone alarm blared, reminding me of my next destination.

Turn off.

A whisp of chamomile drifted across the car to the center console and my phone went silent. I breathed a tiny sigh of relief to know that things really were back to normal. I'd been using my magic for small things ever since I got it back, just to be sure it was still there. I'm sure if Desmond were here, he'd say it was just some kind of stress reaction and would fade with time.

City traffic clogged the roads and my phone blared at me twice more to let me know I was now late. As I sat unmoving behind a taxi, I finally opened my text app and let Duncan know I was on the way. His reply came moments later, and I couldn't help but laugh at his suggestion that I just abandon the car and fly.

Finally, twenty painstaking minutes later, I pulled up to the side of the street outside of Notre Dame. The Green Line MBTA train screeched by on its journey towards Boston College at the end of its route. Pedestrians milled about and some stopped to look at the façade of the building that had bits of police tape still fluttering in the wind. They were no doubt silently questioning what had happened there.

Duncan jogged toward me in a light jacket and jeans from a few parked cars away. "Don't worry, we haven't started without you," he said.

"Glad to know I'm so important," I quipped and popped the trunk of the car. Duncan grabbed one of the bags from within as I hefted the other onto my shoulder.

We walked side by side up to the front door and I tugged the last bits of tape down, stuffing them in my pocket. The interior of Notre Dame was a mess. From obvious water damage to charred and burned flooring, walls, and ceiling. Thankfully, Fire Investigations had released the scene a few days ago.

True to his word, everyone was waiting for me including J.T., Avery, and a bunch of familiar faces from around Authority Headquarters. They all stared at me. I spotted Jacquie's niece and nephew among the group, too. I even noticed Kevin in the back. He flashed me a small smile.

"Are we sure this is going to work?" Avery asked, looking at our surroundings.

"We've confirmed that aside from a couple of support beams in the ceiling, everything else is structurally sound," Duncan said.

Morgan—who I was surprised to see anywhere near paint and power tools—stepped up. I'd only ever seen him sitting behind computers at Authority Headquarters alongside Avery. "My brother owns a furniture business and after I explained what happened, he's donated new tables and chairs."

"Where do we start?" J.T. stepped up, clapping his hands together.

"I think we need to haul everything out that we can first. Then we're going to need to work on demo, taking up the floor and any damaged wall panels," Duncan said.

Jacquie stepped up beside Duncan and I. "Molly can keep him occupied for a few hours, but there's no way we're going to get this done before he comes back."

I grinned at her. "Look around, we've got at least a dozen people with magic. If we work together, we'll be fine."

People dispersed into clusters. I headed behind the bar to assess the damage back there and get started on organizing the top shelf replacements Avery had somehow procured. Duncan joined me, tossing a cleaning rag over his shoulder and offering me a dorky grin.

"What's running through that head of yours?" I teased as I wiped down the shelves that had been spared from the flames.

"I don't know. Just picturing you and me slinging drinks somewhere."

"I think I'd prefer to have someone deliver us drinks instead," I retorted and gestured for him to pass me the box of liquor.

"We both have some vacation time accrued. And it's almost the New Year."

I set the bottle of scotch down and pivoted to look at him. "Are you asking me to go on a vacation with you?"

"Why not?"

"Maybe because we only went on a handful of dates before I broke things off?"

"You settled things with your ex. We saved the embodiment of good magic from being blown up and you got your magic back. Don't you think that deserves a little celebration? And if it happens to be on a beach somewhere with just the two of us, even better. Give yourself permission to be happy for once, Kayla. You deserve it."

I took a deep breath and let it out slowly through my nose. "In case you haven't noticed, I'm not great with the whole self-care thing."

"Never would have guessed," he joked.

"But a trip sounds nice. And seeing where this

goes is definitely something I'm interested in, too." I gestured between us for effect.

"Good."

I couldn't hide the smile that spread across my lips as we got back to work. Behind us, I heard equipment rumble to life as people without magic stripped up the ruined flooring and walls. I turned in time to see Morgan levitating off the ground with no ladder under him as he hammered new support beams in place. He caught me looking and flashed me a toothy grin.

Before long, I felt overlapping bits of magic as the people who'd come together shared their skills to rehabilitate the bar. Someone came through on the opposite side of the bar top and stripped off the burnt paint. I studied the now bare wooden surface, just waiting to be varnished.

"I can do you one better," I whispered as I trailed my fingers across the sanded wood surface.

I closed my eyes and pressed my palms flat to the grain of the wood. I could feel all of the magic around me, weaving in and out of every part of the place, building it back up. I reached inside myself and tugged at my own magic. It was eager to obey. A little part of me believed it had missed me during our involuntary separation. Chamomile enveloped me like a cloud of smoke. It settled my nerves and wafted down toward my fingertips.

Protect it. Keep it clean.

The wood beneath my fingers grew slick for a moment before it hardened. When I opened my eyes, the full length of the bar shone as if it had been lacquered and stained already.

"What did you do?" Jacquie's voice drifted over from the opposite side of the bar.

"Just gave it a little bit of extra protection. Hopefully, it means it's easier to clean." I shrugged. "One of the worst parts of coming here years ago was the bar. It was always kind of sticky by the end of the night, no matter what he did. Maybe now it won't be quite so gross."

Jacquie laughed. "Good thinking. I'm sure he'll appreciate the lack of scrubbing."

At the opposite end of the room, Neveah and Troy handed J.T. light fixtures. Something overhead crackled and electricity arced from the fixture in his hand to the outlet and he jolted on the ladder.

"Maybe let an actual electrician handle that?" I called.

J.T. sucked on the tip of his finger before shaking his head. "I got it."

I heard the front door to the bar open and

everyone froze in place. Molly was supposed to text before she and Jonathan came over to give us enough time to clean up. I pivoted toward the sound of footsteps echoing on the new flooring and my anxiety evaporated when I saw Jonathan's niece, Missy. She stood there, taking in the work we'd managed already.

"This looks amazing," she said and stepped up to the bar. "I saw a couple of guys with trucks pulling up the street. It looks like they've got tables and chairs."

"Right on time," Morgan said, landing on his feet.

Missy reached over the bar and gave me a one-armed embrace. We didn't know each other that well. She'd only bartended a few times for her uncle while she was on school breaks. She'd been too young to do so legally when I'd spent more time here socially.

"Thank you all for organizing this. He won't say it, so I will. This place is my uncle's life and you've all saved it."

"Whether he likes it or not, he's part of the community and we take care of our own," I answered. "Besides, knowing where to go for information is supremely useful when tracking down the bad guys."

"What can I do to help?"

Just then, Morgan returned leading several burly men inside hauling tables and chairs on carts behind them. I gestured to the men and said, "How about you figure out where to set those?"

She flashed me a thumb's up before darting across the room and inserted herself in the mix. Avery wandered over as I gave the bar one last wipe down. She looked more at peace than I'd seen her in a long time.

"Any word on when this big destiny is supposed to hit?"

She shook her head, adjusting her glasses. "No, but I'm ready. I'm not sure what it's going to be exactly. I have a feeling I'll know it when I see it, though."

"Whatever it is, you're going to be great."

She smirked. "Listen to you. Goth girl does pep talks now."

"Only the occasional one."

Before either of us could say more, my phone buzzed with an incoming message from Molly letting us know they were five minutes away. "Okay guys, show time!"

Everyone scrambled to finish up their tasks. It wasn't fully restored to its former glory, but it was habitable and would mean Jonathan had far less work to get the doors open again. The front door opened, and Jonathan's voice preceded his entrance.

"I'm not saying Faneuil Hall isn't a good date place, but it's touristy," he said.

"Well, I appreciate you humoring me," Molly replied as they stepped through the entryway and into the main bar area.

Jonathan stopped short, realizing they were no longer alone. I watched the gears turn in his mind as he processed the fact his bar was no longer a destroyed mess. He turned first to Molly, then to the rest of the group, landing on me last.

"You did this?" The disbelief in his tone tugged at my heart.

"We all did. We take care of our own," I answered, my voice steadier than I'd expected. "You can be a dick sometimes, but you ... this place, it's part of us. We couldn't let you go through this alone."

Jonathan turned his back to us, but he couldn't hide the hitched breaths as he fought to compose himself. Molly simply placed a hand on his arm and waited. When he moved toward us, he blinked to keep his tears in check.

"Well, shit."

"I think the words you're looking for are, thank you," Molly whispered.

"I guess it pays to be part of something after all," he said.

Missy raced across the room to her uncle, flinging her arms around him. He returned the hug and allowed her to lead him around the room, showing off the new and improved features. I leaned against the bar as Molly and Jacquie came to join me.

"You did good Rookie," Jacquie said, patting me on the arm.

"Thanks."

It had been one hell of a year. Nothing had turned out like I'd expected. Yet deep down, I knew I was where I was supposed to be, doing the work I was meant to with the people who had my back. Magic had touched us all in different ways and we would never be the same. And whatever life brought along next, we would face it together.

QUICK AUTHOR'S NOTE

COMING INTO THIS LAST BOOK, I had the

general idea of the premise: Kayla would lose her magic temporarily and Molly would gain it. Originally, I intended that to be the whole plot of the book but as I sat down to write it, I realized that was meant to only be a piece of the puzzle.

And as I contemplated what sort of case might facilitate that magical transfer, I hit on how Kayla would feel without her magic: naked, unimportant, powerless. And that brought me back to the plot of Seasons of Magic book 3, Autumn's Legacy. I hadn't intended to tie in so heavily to that plot but it really worked and it almost felt like coming full circle.

I also knew I needed to wrap up the Kevin/Kayla/Duncan pseudo-triangle before the end of the story. Would you believe I only gave Agent Duncan a first name in this book? I honestly had to go back through the first two and I realized I never actually mentioned his first name. So, hooray for finally setting that right! And it was thanks to one of my Seasons of Magic superfine (and the basis for Agent Cartwright) that I reapplied Kayla had been far more into Kevin than he ever was into her. It allowed me to play with that emotional aspect of what she wants out of life.

And how fun was it to see Jonathan outside the bar? I've got some more fun potential snippets of his and Molly's relationship planned in short form for the future. You'll just have to stay tuned for that.

Speaking of the future, while Kayla's journey is coming to a close, the Seasons of Magic universe is still expanding! I am finally to the point where I can begin sharing the next series in the wider universe: Guardians of Camelot.

The same magical rules apply, but we get to see some new places and faces as a new heroine rises up to take her power back.

TURN *the page for a glimpse of Her Sapphire Blade...*

Sarah Biglow is a *USA Today* bestselling author. She lives in Massachusetts with her husband and son. She is a licensed attorney and spends her days combatting employment discrimination as an Investigator with the Massachusetts Commission Against Discrimination.

You can find an up-to-date list of all my books here